Boarder Patrol

orca sports

Erin Thomas

D0173348

ORCA BOOK PUBLISHERS

Library and Archives Canada Cataloguing in Publication

Thomas, E. L. (Erin L.)
Boarder patrol / written by Erin Thomas.

(Orca sports)

ISBN 978-1-55469-294-1

I. Title. II. Series: Orca sports

PS8639.H572B62 2010   jC813'.6   C2009-906874-5

First published in the United States, 2010
Library of Congress Control Number: 2009940936

Summary: Ryan wants to be a professional snowboarder, but when he
has to choose between promoting his own career and saving his cousin's life,
he does the right thing, despite the loss of a great opportunity.

Orca Book Publishers gratefully acknowledges the support for its
publishing programs provided by the following agencies: the Government
of Canada through the Canada Book Fund and the Canada Council for the
Arts, and the Province of British Columbia through the BC Arts Council
and the Book Publishing Tax Credit.

Cover design by Teresa Bubela
Cover photography by Dreamstime
Author photo by Neil Kinnear and Lesley Chung

Orca Book Publishers
PO Box 5626, Stn. B
Victoria, BC Canada
V8R 6S4

Orca Book Publishers
PO Box 468
Custer, WA USA
98240-0468

www.orcabook.com
Printed and bound in Canada.
Printed on 100% PCW recycled paper.

13 12 11 10 • 4 3 2 1

*For Mom, who didn't laugh when I said
I wanted to write a book for a sports series.*

chapter one

I've always liked this part, sitting on the snow at the top of a mountain, strapping on my snowboard, looking down the run.

"Pretty, isn't it?"

I cranked my neck around to see who was speaking. It was Jamie Clark. The racing helmet she wore muffled her voice, so I hadn't recognized it right away. Her long brown ponytail was a dead giveaway though. Not that I needed it. I could pick out her jacket and board and the way she stood, from all the way up in the chairlift.

So could my cousin, Kevin. He was the one usually riding the lifts with me, rolling his eyes while I pointed out Jamie. He was more like a brother to me, really, especially now that my parents had moved away. I had stayed behind, living with Kevin and his parents so I could finish high school close to the mountains. I'd given up a lot for boarding. I wondered, sometimes, if I'd made the right choice.

I spent all my time outside of school and work riding my board. I had no social life to speak of. There were good parts though, and hanging out with Jamie was one of the good parts.

"I guess," I said.

I'm sixteen. Somehow I thought there'd be some deep-seated knowledge kicking in by now, making small talk with girls feel as natural as riding a board. It hasn't happened.

Jamie didn't answer. She just lifted off her helmet and sat down beside me.

"You going down?" I asked. Which was clever, given that we were sitting at the top of a run, and she was strapping on her board.

She grinned. "Thought I might. Want to race?"

"Race?" I knew Jamie went in for boardercross racing sometimes, but that wasn't really my thing. Boardercross is like motocross on a snowboard; riders race down the hill, and it's more about speed than style. If you can stay in control and not get knocked over by the other guy, you've got a shot at winning. I stuck to the slopestyle competitions, where it's what you do on the hill that matters, not how fast you get down it. I like to do tricks. In boardercross, "showboating" costs you speed. In slopestyle, it wins you points.

She nodded. "It's a time-honored tradition. Two competitors start down the same run at the same time, and the one who reaches the end first wins."

"Funny girl."

"Come on, Ryan. There's a race this Sunday, and you know they always use this run. I could use the practice. You're not going to compete, are you?" She knew I never raced boardercross, so she didn't bother waiting for me to speak. "You can help me, then. Let's go."

She hopped up on her board, slid around and dug her toe edge in, facing me. She held out a mittened hand.

"Loser buys the winner hot chocolate?" I let her tug me up.

We slid to the drop-off. I tugged my goggles into place and tightened my helmet strap.

The run we were standing on, Funnel Run, started out wide and then got narrow halfway down. After that, the course was broken up with jumps and turns. Of course, in boardercross, that's when the interesting stuff happens. The racers crash into one another and cut each other off, trying to get ahead.

I had no intention of bodychecking Jamie. She was a lot smaller than me. I'd just have to nail my lead by the halfway point.

"One," she said, eyeing me.

"Two," I said.

She took off, buying a board-length lead by the time she called "Three."

chapter two

I tucked, going for speed as I dropped into the hill. I ride goofy—right foot forward. Jamie rides regular—left foot forward. So we were facing each other as I shot past her and waved.

I threw in a couple of *S* curves, barely touching my edges to the snow, just enough to stay in control. The wind blasted my helmet.

Jamie cut down a steep slope, angling toward me. I thought she was going to check me, so I tucked again and got out of the way. She's not big, but even a hundred pounds of dive-bombing snowboarder is to be avoided.

Boardercross. Not my sport.

She had put me off my course, and, as we headed into the narrow bit, she had the more direct line down the hill. I edged closer, crowding her, but she didn't give.

I scanned ahead. There was another boarder on the hill. We'd have to avoid him. He was well past the narrows, so no problem. If I forced Jamie left, though, she'd have to take a jump to avoid him. I might be able to gain some ground while she was in the air.

I moved in, forcing her up the hill. She had to give ground or risk coming too close to the other boarder. She went for a straight jump, not a lot of air, trying for distance rather than height. In the meantime, I crouched low and zoomed ahead.

Jamie rode high on a curve, trying to come down ahead of me again, but it cost her speed.

One of my favorite jumps was at the bottom of this run. It's why I wanted to ride down it in the first place. And I had time. Jamie was way behind me now.

I took the jump, rather than riding straight to the finish. I should have played it straight, like Jamie had done on the other jump, but in the end, I couldn't resist. I had the speed. I knew I could nail it.

And I admit, knowing that Jamie was right behind me and had a good view of whatever I did provided some pretty decent motivation. I caught my heel edge to give me the height I needed and turned the jump into a flip. When I was upside down, I opened up and turned it into a twist. Backside rodeo. I landed tight and rode away, feeling good.

And there was Jamie, waiting for me at the bottom of the hill, clapping. "Nice," she said. "But I still won the race." She pulled her helmet off.

"How did you—?"

"Some of us don't waste time with fancy tricks when we're racing," she said. She grinned. "I'm ready for my hot chocolate now. Do you need to radio in or whatever before you go on break?"

I blinked at her for a second before I remembered—I was working. Volunteering, technically, but being a Junior Ski Patrol volunteer got me a free lift pass, which I needed.

"Uh, no," I said. All the patrol ever used me for was rolling up safety fence, and that wasn't exactly urgent. Only the adults, the real patrollers, looked after the people who got hurt on the hill.

"Then let's go," she said.

"Excuse me. Do you have a moment?" It was the other snowboarder, the one we had passed on the hill. I groaned. Was he going to give us a hard time? Sure, we shouldn't have been racing, but it wasn't like we didn't know what we were doing.

I turned half away from him so he might not notice my ski-patrol armband. A bad report might cost me my lift pass.

"That was some nice boarding," he said. "My name's Ted Travis. I put together videos. Sports footage."

"Thanks," I said. Then I blurted out, "I know who you are." Ted Travis was the videographer behind some of the best boarding videos I'd seen.

His mouth twitched up in an almost smile. "You think you could do a repeat of that little stunt you pulled?" he asked.

I stared at him as his words sunk in. "I know I could," I said finally. There was a "sir" somewhere back there, in my mouth, but I didn't let it out. I didn't want to sound too eager, in case I was wrong about why he was asking the question.

"How about you, miss? You ride a lot?"

"I do," Jamie said. She looked puzzled, but I knew what was coming. Or I hoped

I did. My mouth was dry, and my palms felt sweaty inside my gloves. If he wanted us to be in one of his videos...that was good. That was amazing.

If Ted chose Jamie and me for a video, it would all be worthwhile. It would mean that I had been right to stay behind when my parents moved to Winnipeg. It would mean that I was a serious snowboarder with a serious shot at having a career, not just some whiny kid who got mad at his dad and bailed on him when things got hard.

"I was just about to take a break, but why don't we meet at the east lift in twenty minutes? We'll take a run over to the terrain park together. I'd like to see what else the two of you can do," Ted said.

I took the card he handed me and shook his hand. My dad had taught me how to shake hands—firm enough so no one thinks you're a pushover, not so firm that it seems like you've got something to prove. Ted nodded at me before turning away.

After Ted left, I turned to Jamie, grinning so wide I thought my face might split. "Can you believe this?"

She was staring, puzzled, at the card in her hand. "It's a good thing?"

"Are you kidding? It's—," I started, but I was interrupted by a squeal from the radio I wore strapped to my chest under my coat.

"Ryan, do you copy?" It was Allison, the patrol leader.

"Sure. I, uh, copy," I said into the microphone. I always felt like such a nerd, talking on the radio.

"Then get yourself down to the patrol hut right now."

chapter three

She was gone, without so much as an *over and out*. Which really wasn't like Allison.

Jamie agreed to meet me by the east chair in fifteen minutes, not twenty. That would give us a chance to talk before meeting Ted.

All the way down to the patrol hut, my mind raced. A Ted Travis video. Videos meant exposure, and exposure meant sponsors. It all added up to a chance to turn professional someday.

When I got to the patrol hut, Allison was waiting. "I had a report that you were racing in uniform, Ryan. Is that true? Because you know the rule on reckless skiing."

Allison, obviously, is a skier, not a boarder. She has trouble translating plank-talk.

"It wasn't reckless," I said.

"Racing down a public run and pulling an invert maneuver isn't reckless?"

Seriously, who uses words like that? Invert maneuver. It was a flip. "I was in control," I said. Just at the edge of it, sometimes, but I know what I'm doing. "There was only one other person on that run, and he didn't complain."

She pressed her lips together. "Be that as it may, I'm going to have to write this up. This is one strike against you, Ryan. You don't want to get three."

Not if it was going to cost me my lift pass, I didn't. I had a part-time job at a gas station, but that money went to room and board, and to my college fund.

I wasn't going to let Allison know any of that though.

"Are we clear, Ryan?"

I hate it when people use your name all the time when they're talking to you. A smart remark was in my mouth, ready to come out. I could taste it, but I didn't say it.

Dad used to tell me my smart mouth would land me in trouble. Funny thing, when in a way it was *his* smart mouth that cost so many people their jobs. Some people think my dad was a hero. Some think he should be burned at the stake for giving the car-battery plant a reason to pull out of town. Job loss versus water pollution; always a tough call for the corporate whistleblower.

Anyhow, I was learning to keep my mouth shut when I needed to. I just stared at Allison until she nodded.

It felt good to leave the hut and step out into the cold again. I had ten minutes to get down to the east lift to meet Jamie. I could blow off some steam on the way down.

There's a rack outside the patrol hut where patrollers can leave their skis and boards. I normally brought my board inside, but today I had been in a hurry, so I had left it on the rack.

Now it was gone.

chapter four

I stomped back into the patrol hut. "Did you move my board?"

Allison glanced up from the stack of patient call reports. "What?"

"My snowboard. It was on the rack. Did you move it?"

"I haven't left the patrol hut since you were just in here, Ryan."

She had a point. Still, a normal person would have just said no.

"It's gone," I said.

I must have looked as upset as I felt, because some of her frown lines smoothed away. "Calm down, Ryan. Are you sure you left it on the rack?"

"Yes, I'm sure."

"I'll come and help you look."

We searched all around the hut. Then we searched the ski racks in front of the lodge. With two of us looking, we could have covered the area twice as fast. We didn't work quickly though; we worked carefully. We searched every rack twice. In the end, there was really no doubt.

"Someone must have taken it," I said. Saying it out loud made it real. Theft was a problem at any resort, and this had been a bad year for it at Salmon Valley.

"Possibly," Allison admitted. "Look, there's always some gear left over from the ski swaps. You can look in the storage closet and see if there's anything you can use to get you through today."

The stuff in the storage closet was left over for a reason. Clunky boards, antique bindings. Straight skis, for Pete's sake.

Allison had been nice though, helping me look for my board. She didn't have to do that. So I bit back the smart remark that jumped into my mouth and thanked her instead.

"You're welcome, Ryan," she said. "I hope your board shows up."

I didn't hold out a lot of hope. It wasn't like I could afford to replace it either. I didn't like the thought of taking a few hundred out of my bank account. I was going to be iffy on tuition next year as it was. But that was better than losing a season. Snowboarding was my future.

I rummaged through the storage closet. One board was usable, barely. It would get me where I needed to go.

My cousin Kevin wouldn't let me down. He never did.

If a guy is willing to share his room with you so you don't have to move to

Winnipeg, he'll probably be willing to lend you a snowboard. Or so I hoped.

I was already late for my meeting with Jamie and Ted. They'd be halfway up the east chair by now, if they hadn't waited for me.

The board Allison had lent me felt sluggish, like I was riding on plywood. On this board, there was no point auditioning. The best I could do was catch up to Ted, explain what had happened, and ask for another shot.

At any other ski hill than Salmon Valley, I'd have been out of luck. But I wasn't on any other ski hill. Kevin and I had been coming here since we were kids. He was working as a lift attendant this year.

I was late, but if Kevin helped me out, at least I'd have a fighting chance.

chapter five

Kevin is a year older than me. At the start of the season, I'd asked if he could get me hired on as a liftie too, but he said it wasn't a good idea. The money wasn't that great, and he knew I wanted to spend my time riding, not standing in one place.

He had been right. Kevin rarely rode anymore. I missed boarding with him.

It was weird. Even though we lived together now, we weren't close like we used to be. Maybe it was *because* we lived together. When you share a room with somebody, you start taking your personal space where you can get it.

Kevin was in a small hut at the top of the Bearclaw chairlift. On a beginner run like the Bearclaw, there's a good chance that the little runoff slope is going to be the steepest hill the rookies deal with all day. Kevin told me there were more pile-ups coming off the Bearclaw chair than on the rest of the lifts combined.

As I approached, a boarder got tangled up with the skis of the girl riding the lift with him. They slid down the hill as one wobbly unit and crashed at the bottom. The next chair was coming up fast.

Kevin stopped it just in time. The chair swung back and forth, four skiers packed tight, like gum in a package. Kevin stomped out of the lift hut to hike down the hill and untangle the pileup. I got there at the same time he did.

The boy saw me first. "Wow, you guys are fast," he said.

Oh yeah. Ski-patrol armband. "Are you okay?" I asked. They were moving, and I could see that they were fine. It just seemed polite to ask. Allison would have been proud.

I helped the girl up and retrieved a ski pole for her, even though I really didn't have time. By then, Kevin had the snowboarder back on his feet. "Clear the ramp," Kevin said. Man of few words. He turned and started back up the short hill to the lift line, waving to me over his shoulder. "Hey, cuz," he said.

"Can I borrow your board?" I asked. Kevin had bought a new one this year. It was the same make as mine, only longer. I'd like to know how he got the money. Then again, Kevin had no intention of going to college, so he had no reason to save.

He shrugged, still walking uphill. "Sure. What happened to yours?"

"I think it got stolen."

"Seriously?" His gaze made it down to the ground, to the ancient scabby board I had borrowed.

"Kev, it's important, or I wouldn't ask."

He waved a hand. "I said yes." He reached into the lift hut and pulled out his shiny black board. "Catch," he said.

Only Kevin would send a new board shooting downhill. I managed to get in front of it just in time. "Thanks. You rock."

"No sweat," he said. "Leave me that tray you've got there, in case I need it."

Did I mention that Kevin's my favorite cousin?

By the time I finally made it to the terrain park and found Jamie and Ted, I was nearly half an hour late. Jamie was sliding down the long rail as I approached, the toe side of her board barely skimming the rail's metal surface. It was a tough move. I'm pretty good on a rail—a long strip of metal like a stair railing, sticking out of the snow for boarders to slide down—but I hadn't mastered that move yet.

Ted paced near the rail as Jamie finished her stunt and sat down to take her board off for the walk back up the hill.

I slid up behind Ted. "I'm really sorry I'm late, sir," I said. Funny how that "sir" came out no problem, now that I needed him to forgive me for being late.

"Your loss, kid," he said. His tone made it sound final.

No way I was watching my chance slip away. "My board was stolen. I had to borrow one."

That, at least, earned me a glance. "Someone loaned you a brand-new Burton?"

"My cousin." I didn't tell him that it was a different size than mine, or that I wasn't used to riding it. I didn't want to give him any reason not to let me ride for him.

"Your cousin must like you."

That wasn't what we were here to talk about. I waited.

"What the hell," he said. "Let's see what you can do with your cousin's board then."

I nodded, trying to look confident. Kevin's board is great, but it's not mine. It's longer and handles differently. I didn't

25

exactly have time to do a trial run. I needed to make the first time count.

"On the rail?" I asked, since that was what Jamie was setting up for.

"Sure," he said, sounding like he didn't much care either way.

I bent down to unfasten my bindings, watching out of the corner of my eye as Jamie approached the rail again. She didn't bother to swerve on her approach, just headed straight for it and hopped up at the last second. She balanced over the rail, the tip of her board barely touching it. It almost looked like she was floating down the hill on air, beside the rail. Nice.

I wasn't going to try that my first time, not on a board that was longer than I was used to. With my luck, I'd misjudge it and end up with a mouthful of rail. I fastened my board, still thinking about what to do.

I tucked to build up some decent speed heading into the rail, then landed on it right foot forward, with my board running lengthwise along the rail. Halfway down the rail I crouched, and then popped up into a quick jump. I twisted, landing again to finish the rail-riding switch—wrong foot forward. For me, that's the left, which meant my back was to Ted as I came off the rail. Not ideal, but I made a clean finish and curved around to face him.

He nodded, which I took as my cue to keep going. Jamie was already walking back up the hill. I unfastened my bindings and did the same.

We took turns riding the rail for a while. I made a mental note to wax Kevin's snowboard for him when I was done to cover the scratches on the bottom. Rails are tough on boards.

I eventually got brave enough to try the "float" thing Jamie had done. I could do it easily on my board, but I flubbed it on Kevin's. The end of Kevin's board was two inches farther away than the end of the board I was used to. I landed on my face.

"It's not a blooper reel, kid," Ted yelled. I gritted my teeth.

After a while, he called us over. "Not bad," he said. "I had a chance to see Jamie hit some jumps earlier, but I'd like to go back to that. Then maybe try the pipe."

We worked with him for almost an hour, trying different jumps in the terrain park. Then we spent another twenty minutes in the half pipe. Jamie was great. I was okay. Maybe. I could manage the basics well enough on Kevin's board, but whenever I tried anything really impressive, I bailed. After a while, I figured it was better to stick to the basics and look competent than to spend the entire session on my butt.

Jamie managed to get close to me at one point while we waited our turn to drop into the pipe. "What's wrong with you? Why were you so late? And why are you holding back?"

"Long story," I said. She frowned, but there was no time for anything else.

Jamie didn't know the look of my board like I did hers. Why would she? This was clearly a one-way obsession.

When we finished up, Ted promised to be in touch. He didn't say when, or whether we'd done okay. I wanted to ask him so badly that my teeth hurt from biting my question back, but I just shook his hand and said thanks, trying to act professional. I knew my ride hadn't been good.

"Want to go for that hot chocolate now?" Jamie asked.

I really didn't. She'd want to talk about our tryout, and I wasn't in the mood. I shook my head. "Gotta return my cousin's board," I said.

"Your cousin's—" Her mouth gaped open like a fish. "That's why you were boarding like a rook. What happened to yours?"

"Just felt like a change," I lied. Why get into it? There was nothing she could do. I left before she could ask me any more questions.

I headed back to Kevin's lift hut, but the liftie there told me Kevin had already gone down to the chalet. When I finally caught up with him, he grinned. "Got something to show you, cuz," he said.

I followed him out to the truck. Kevin had bought a used Chevy Silverado shortly after the start of the season. Like I said, he always seemed to have money. More money than you'd expect, given how much he made at the ski hill. One of these days I'd have to ask him how he did it.

"Toss my board in the back," he said.

I was just about to do that when I saw what was already there—my board, in the back of Kevin's pickup truck. "How did you find it?"

He shrugged. "Just gotta know who to ask."

That left me feeling uneasy. "Was it stolen?"

"Call it misplaced," he said. "Look, I can't really get into it. Just be happy you've got it back, and don't leave it lying around again, okay?"

That was a yes. So Kevin knew who was nabbing boards at the hill. I wondered how he had convinced them to give it back. "Okay," I said. For now, I was happy to have it back. Maybe when Ted called, I could convince him to let me try out for him again. I'd get the truth out of Kevin another time. We'd never kept secrets from one another before.

chapter six

Sweep. Last run. Hill to myself.

This was the part I liked best. Even though we couldn't do any real riding, even though we had to go slow and look in the trees and over the sides of all the runs, there was something great about knowing the last set of tracks on a run were mine. It felt like trespassing. Better—it felt like I owned the mountain.

We'd had fresh snow that afternoon. With evening's temperature drop, it had settled into a light crust that crunched beneath my board when I mapped out turns on fresh ground. I'd been assigned to sweep Bridge Run. Not a great run for snowboarders, because of the long flat bit where I'd have to take one boot out of the binding and skate, but I didn't mind. It was one of the more isolated runs on the hill. Narrow too, and quiet, with thick trees on either side and a steep drop-off to one side of the trail.

Allison never swept this hill. I didn't mind being in the woods at night.

I reached the bridge, a long flat bit where the run crossed over a frozen creek. The bridge was built of wood, with high side rails and one of those fake-grass carpets over it. Of course, it was covered in snow now. I only knew about the carpet from riding my bike here in the off-season.

I slid as far as my momentum carried me and then sat down to unfasten my right foot from the binding. "Hill's closing," I called out. We were supposed to yell that periodically, in case anyone had gone off the trail and out of sight.

There was no answer other than the crunch of snow and rustle of my snowpants as I stood. My breath fogged in front of my face.

I crossed the bridge: push and glide, push and glide. Like lining up for a chair-lift. The trail angled down shortly after the bridge, so I sat to refasten my binding. That was when I noticed the snowboard track veering off from the main trail into the brush.

"Hello?" I called. No reason to think anyone was there. Probably just some kid goofing off earlier in the day.

But I was pretty sure the rider wouldn't have connected with another trail. Not going in that direction. And I didn't see any scuffed-up snow to indicate where someone might have climbed back up.

"Crap." Instead of putting my snowboard back on, I took it off and crossed the run to where the snowboard track led off into the bush. The smooth, flat track followed the curve of the hill down, past the reach of the trail lights. From where I was, it looked like dark trees and shadows swallowed it up. Double crap.

"Hello? Anyone there?"

No answer. I'd have killed for a flashlight just then.

That was when I remembered I had one—sort of. Junior patrollers don't carry full first-aid kits like the adult patrollers do, but we have little emergency kits. I usually stuffed mine in a pocket, where it made one more annoying bulge, like the radio. The kit had a mini-Maglite in it though.

I tugged off my gloves and dug it out. My fingers grew cold and useless pretty fast, but I got the flashlight out and turned it on. I didn't bother with the wrist strap— my fingers were too stiff. Someone had made sure the batteries were fresh. Lovely, lovely Allison with her lovely checklists and charts and equipment inventories. I'd have to thank her later.

Allison. I fumbled for the radio button. "Er—patrol call?"

"Go ahead, Ryan," she said.

"It might be nothing. I don't know. I thought I saw tracks off Bridge Run, just past the bridge. I'm going to check it out," I said.

The silence lasted long enough that I was sure I'd surprised her. "Good work, Ryan. Do you need assistance?" she asked.

"No. Not yet. I'll let you know if— if I find anything."

"Roger. Allison out."

I resisted the urge to add "ten-four, good buddy." It didn't feel like a time for goofing around.

Armed with the tiny flashlight, gloves back on, I worked my way down the side of the hill, going tree to tree. Once I passed out of the reach of the hill lights, the forest closed in on me. It was a cloudy night, just my luck, so no moonlight, nothing to reflect off the snow except my small circle of light. No sound except the crunch of my footsteps as I sank in knee-high snow with each step.

One step sank deeper, and I grabbed for a tree trunk as my leg sank to thigh level. Off the hard-packed trail, there was always the danger of ending up in a tree well, a dangerous patch of loose, deep snow in the shelter of a tree. I pulled back.

"Hello?" I called again, shining my flashlight in a slow arc.

I heard a groan.

chapter seven

I dropped my Maglite. The darkness was complete, except for a tiny glow under the snow by my left foot. I knelt and fumbled for it, nearly crying with relief when my fingers closed on something hard and cylindrical.

This time, I looped the Maglite's strap around my wrist. "Where are you?" I called into the darkness. The groan had come from downhill and to my right, I thought. I moved step by step, testing the snow as I went, aiming my flashlight wide. After each step, I stopped to listen. Had I imagined it? Maybe it was an animal.

Then I saw it: a dark shape huddled around a tree, half-buried in snow.

My mouth went dry. I forced myself to move slowly, not to run up to him, because that's not how you approach a patient. Slow and steady—I could hear Allison's voice in my head, speaking the way she had during our first-aid training.

I didn't want to approach him at all. I wanted to run away. A dark, mysterious shape in the woods at night is nobody's idea of a good time, least of all mine. The flashlight beam wavered. It took me a moment to realize that it was because my hands were shaking. I forced myself to keep moving, one step, then another. It was what my dad would have done.

I knelt beside him, sinking a few inches into the snow. He was curled around the tree, facing away from me. "Can you hear me?" No answer. "I'm Ryan, with the

Ski Patrol. I'm, uh, just going to see if you're okay." I touched his shoulder. I knew not to shake him or move him in case he had a spinal injury. I remembered that much from the first-aid course.

I leaned over him, aiming my light at his face. His skin was waxy-pale and blue around the lips. The eye I could see was half-open and rolled back. "Gah!" I jumped back. My heart banged at my chest, like it was trying to escape.

He looked dead. I was in the woods with a dead guy, with one puny flashlight between me and the dark. So much for bravery. I felt about five years old. I wanted my dad.

I took a deep breath. My hands shook. It was hard to get a glove off. I had to use my teeth. I held my hand in front of his nose and mouth, since I wasn't sure I could bend far enough around him to check properly. After a few seconds, I felt it—a stirring of warmer air against my skin.

"Oh, thank god." I'm not even religious, but I was pretty sure I meant it.

I radioed Allison, telling her what I had found and where we were. I sank back into my heels. Someone was coming. It was okay that I didn't know what to do.

The man's back faced me. I shivered. It was growing colder by the second. He'd been in that snow a long time. Without really thinking about it, I shrugged out of my jacket and spread it over him, tucking it under his back as best I could. "I don't know if you can hear me," I said. "It's Ryan again. I just wanted you to know that help's coming. I called the Ski Patrol. Allison's in charge tonight; she's the patrol leader. Trust me, she knows what she's doing...probably has the entire textbook memorized. Hell, maybe she wrote it, I don't know."

I was babbling, but I didn't care. I wasn't even talking for his sake so much as just to hear a voice in the darkness, even if it was my own. I held the flashlight tight and imagined warmth coming off it. I was cold without my jacket.

It wasn't long before I heard the patrol coming. Allison called me, and I shouted back until they found us. I stood back and watched while they checked the man over. They put a stiff, white cervical collar on him and tied him to a spine board with straps.

Once he was loaded into the sled, a few of the patrollers rigged some kind of pulley system and hauled him out of the trees. I was tired and numb by the time we all reached the hill.

"Here," Allison said, handing me my jacket. I put it on, but it was damp with snow and as chilled through as I was. I didn't bother with the zipper. My hands felt too clumsy for that. "You did well, Ryan."

I was slow getting down the rest of Bridge Run, partly because I still had to sweep it and partly because my body just didn't want to move fast. Allison hung back with me, even though I could tell she wanted to rush down to the patrol hut and supervise. I thought that was nice of her.

By the time we got to the hut, the ambulance was already there. Allison skied right up to the stretcher, so I followed. One of the paramedics greeted her by name.

"Hey, Jerry," she said. "How's he doing?"

The paramedic gave her an update that involved a lot of words I didn't understand. Then he looked at me and frowned in a way that I was getting used to. "You're Robert Sullivan's kid," he said.

I raised my chin. No point denying it. I look exactly like my dad, and I live in a small town. I waited to see what Jerry, the medic, had to say. A lot of it would depend on whether any of his friends or family had lost their jobs as a result of what my dad did.

"Ryan's one of our junior patrollers, Jerry," Allison said. "He's the one who found the patient."

"I went to school with your dad. Shame what happened," Jerry said.

I shrugged. "He's doing okay now," I said.

Jerry clapped me on the shoulder. "He's a brave man. How about you? You looking to go into ambulance work?"

Not freaking likely. I knew what happened when you let other people's problems become your own. I wasn't looking to make a career out of it. "Not a chance," I said. I didn't realize until after I'd said it how it would sound—like I was insulting Jerry for his career choice. "I mean, I don't think so." I tried again. "I'm really more interested in snowboarding." I saw that look on his face then, the one grown-ups get when they think you're a silly little kid with big dreams, but at least I wasn't insulting anybody now.

Allison frowned. I felt bad, since she'd been so nice to me, but mostly I just wanted to go home. Kevin would have finished closing the lifts by now. "My cousin's waiting for me," I said. "Okay if I go?"

Allison nodded. "I'll sign you out," she said. She forgot to use my name.

By the time I got to the parking lot, I was wiped. I crawled into the cab of Kevin's pickup truck. It was only a fifteen-minute drive home, a bit more than an hour on foot. Tonight, I was glad I didn't have to walk it. "Thanks for waiting," I said.

He nodded.

Nice thing about Kevin: he's never been one to ask a lot of questions. I leaned back and closed my eyes, he drove and that was all.

I thought I'd fall asleep as soon as my head hit the pillow. It didn't happen. My brain felt buzzed, like I'd had too much caffeine. I found myself wishing Winnipeg was a couple of hours behind Kamloops instead of a couple of hours ahead. I wanted to talk to my dad.

I'd saved a man's life. That was the sort of thing a person ought to be able to tell someone about.

"Kev? You awake?"

"Yeah," he said.

"Did you hear what happened on the hill?"

I heard him roll over. "Saw the ambulance. Figured you guys were involved," he said. "Guy hurt bad?"

"Pretty bad. Thought he was dead at first." I paused. "I was the one who found him." There was no way to say that without sounding like either a show-off or a baby.

"Seriously? Guess he's lucky then, eh?" Somehow, Kevin managed not to make me feel like either. "You okay?" he said. "You were quiet in the truck."

"Yeah." I felt like I should thank him, but he would ask me what for. "For listening" was the sappiest possible answer. By the time I settled on "Good night," he was already snoring.

It wasn't until much later that I remembered I had questions to ask him. They could wait though. Maybe he was right.

The important thing was that I had my board back. Did it really matter how or why? I trusted Kevin. Didn't I?

chapter eight

I caught a ride back to the hill with Kevin the next morning. I wasn't scheduled for patrol. I just wanted to get some runs in before my shift at the gas station. Just as well I wasn't patrolling. It was a little too soon after the body-in-the-woods thing.

When I took a break for lunch, I saw Kevin. Not at his truck, but walking through the parking lot, a snowboard tucked under his arm. Not his own board.

I hung back and watched.

He carried the board to a white van and knocked on the back window. Someone opened it, and Kevin passed him the board. Then he left.

I stared. There was no way Kevin was stealing. He wouldn't be involved in something like that. There had to be an explanation.

I waited until he left the van, and then I hurried to catch up with him. Kevin's legs are longer than mine.

"So, what was that all about?" I asked.

He slouched along, neither slowing down for me nor hurrying to get away. "All what about?"

"The snowboard you took to the van. Whose was that?"

He looked at me sideways. "Friend forgot his board, that's all. I just brought it back for him."

Right. That made sense. Obviously. But my mouth wouldn't shut up. "So this doesn't have anything to do with...how you got my board back?"

Kevin shrugged.

I hated being brushed off, and I especially hated it coming from Kevin. I took two fast steps to get in front of him and then turned around, blocking his path. "What's going on, Kev?"

"You got a problem?" That wasn't like Kevin at all. Well, it was, but not when he was talking to me.

"Should I?"

He moved to step around me, but I didn't let him. "Piss off, Ryan."

I blinked. Kevin hadn't ever told me to piss off in his life. "Piss off" was something that we told other people to do. "Not until you tell me what's going on."

"I just did."

Someone approached us from behind Kevin. An older guy, maybe in his twenties. Tall. I expected him to keep walking, but he stopped. "Anything wrong, Kevin?"

he asked, glancing at me. He had a close-trimmed beard along his jawline. Looked dumb, if you asked me. His jaw stuck out too far already, so why draw attention to it?

"Nothing's wrong. My cousin here saw me carrying your snowboard. He seemed to think it might be stolen."

The guy's eyebrow shot up. "But it's not stolen if you were bringing it back to me, right?" He clapped Kevin on the shoulder. "Thanks for that, by the way. I owe you a coffee. So, no problem here?"

"Guess not," I said. I felt like a jerk. I wasn't going to apologize though. Not in front of some friend of Kevin's that I'd never even met.

The guy nodded at me, then headed back to his van, leaving Kevin and me glaring at each other.

"You have to admit, it looked bad," I said.

"I don't have to admit anything," Kevin said.

I watched him go, wondering who had replaced my cousin with a jerk.

Jamie caught up with me on the hill later. I had hiked up to have another go at the tabletop. I wasn't paying attention, or she might not have caught me. My brain was still back at that white van.

She hit me with a snowball. It didn't hurt, but it got my attention. "Hey, Ryan. Did you register for the comp yet?" she asked, grinning as she rode closer.

"Comp?" The lip of the jump was a bit deeper on the left. I'd try to hit it there, next time.

"The Burton Slopestyle. Saturday?" She put her hands on her hips. "You forgot, didn't you? I don't know what's with you. First you're late for Ted, then you forget a competition. Registration's today."

"Thanks," I said. I meant for the reminder. She was right. I shouldn't have forgotten. It was a big competition, with sponsorship and money attached, and slopestyle was my event. It wasn't like I didn't know it was coming. I just hadn't realized it was so soon. "Are you in it?"

She looked at me strangely. "Of course."

So why was she reminding me? If I didn't show, there was a good chance Jamie would clean up. Her mind didn't work like that though.

I pointed at the tabletop, feeling like I should offer her something in return. "Hit it on the left. It's a bit deeper."

She nodded. "I heard from Ted," she said, offhand. She left it hanging. That was my opening to say that I had too. Except I hadn't.

"That was fast," I said. Except it wasn't, really. It had been a couple days. And if he'd called Jamie but not me, that was probably all the answer I needed. Suddenly angry, I started to slide. Jamie put a mittened hand on my arm to stop me.

"What?"

"He didn't call you?"she said. She blinked a couple of times, like she was surprised.

"Obviously."

She let me go. "He probably will."

I shrugged.

"It's not going to be that great, anyhow. Slopestyle, but on the back of the mountain, not in the park. He wants rocks and trees and cliffs instead of jumps and rails. Back-forty stuff."

She let her voice trail off. It sounded great, and she had to know it.

"Doesn't matter," I said. "I'd better go get my registration in." But the competition was a tiny thing beside the chance that Ted had offered.

I felt her eyes on me as I headed down the hill.

The damned white van was still there when I got down to the main chalet. It was parked in a different place now, but I recognized the license plate. To make things even better, while I watched, some guy I didn't recognize carried a pair of skis out to the van and shoved them in the back. He was wearing snowboard boots.

Kevin could take his cover story and shove it. No one had ever accused me of being stupid.

That wasn't entirely true. There was this incident with a supply teacher in grade-nine math class...but really, how obvious did these guys want to be? Same van, different people carrying skis and boards out all the time. It was like they were trying to get caught.

My cell phone has a camera in it. I waited until the guy left, then I wandered over to the van, hoping for a glance inside. I held my phone low in my hand and snapped a picture of the license plate as I approached.

There didn't seem to be anyone in the front seat. I walked up to the driver's-side door and tried to open it. It was locked.

I pretended to fumble in my pockets for the keys, in case anyone was watching. I tried the other doors too, but they were all locked. The side windows were tinted and the back ones were completely mirrored. I couldn't get a good look in the back.

What was I trying to prove, anyhow? That Kevin had lied to me? It didn't take pictures and proof to tell me that. Kevin was stealing. Kevin didn't trust me. I wasn't sure which bothered me more. Disgusted, I turned my back on the van.

Kevin was standing behind me. "Get an eyeful?" he asked. He shoved me into the van door. "I told you to stay away." Clearly, I was still dealing with evil-jerk Kevin rather than regular friendly Kevin.

"You told me a lot of things. Like that you didn't know who took my board."

"Is that what this is about?" He was bigger than me. I'd never felt it more than I did now; he towered over me as he spoke. "Grow up. The only reason you're not getting the crap beat out of you right now is that I told the other guys I'd handle it. You of all people should know better than to stick your nose where it doesn't belong."

Meaning that my dad would still have a job if he hadn't been so quick to draw conclusions. And talk about them.

"At least I'm not a thief, Kevin."

"No, just a spoiled brat. Get out of my face. You can find another ride to work." He sounded like he really hated me.

Honestly, I think I liked it better when he was shoving me into the van door.

"Gladly." I left, wondering exactly when things had gotten so screwed up between us.

chapter nine

I sat at the top of the hill with Jamie, waiting for our numbers to be called. I'd had to trade a patrol shift to get the time off for the slopestyle competition, but that had been easy. Since I pretty much lived at the hill, I was happy to take the Saturday night shifts that no one wanted. Getting rid of a few hours on a Saturday afternoon was never a problem.

I'd found out a little more about the guy I found in the woods too. Turns out he'd been high on something when he'd gone off the trail. The file was supposed to be all hush-hush, but of course the whole patrol knew about it. I wondered if he'd bought the stuff at the hill or brought his own. Not that it mattered, but because of the whole thing with Kevin, I was feeling a little more tuned in than usual to what went on at the hill.

Jamie was stretching. Right there in the snow, she spread her legs out in a V. Then she leaned over to grab her right boot with both mittened hands, bringing her forehead to her knee. The motion pulled her snow-pants tight in key places. Was she trying to stay loose for her ride or distract me so I messed up mine? If she kept it up, both were likely.

She leaned over her left leg, and then stood, reaching her arms behind her back. "You should stretch too, you know."

"Uh, thanks, no. Already did." Yeah, last year in phys-ed class, when we did a unit on it.

"I mean it. I'd never have done a gymnastics competition without warming up and stretching. This is no different. You could tear a muscle."

"Gymnastics?" It explained a lot, actually. Jamie's flexibility, the graceful way she rode. I had a mental image of her in skin-tight spandex. Not helpful. I pulled my brain back and tried to focus, planning my run.

On the plus side, she had distracted me from thinking about Kevin.

And with that, suddenly I was thinking of Kevin again. We hadn't spoken in days. Tricky, since we shared a room, but stubbornness was a family trait.

I eyed Jamie, hoping she would do that stretching thing again. If I was going to blow this competition anyhow, I'd rather do it distracted by a pretty girl than by an angry cousin.

My number was called. I stood, full of that jittery adrenaline-overdose feeling. My hands shook a little. But no more than usual before a competition.

"Break a leg," Jamie called.

"What?"

She laughed and waved, and then it was time for me to head to the starting line.

There was a choice to make right off the bat: bumps on my left or a gap jump on my right. I can do the bumps by pivoting my back foot, but it looks messy. I'm stronger with jumps, so I went with those. It's always a tough call, with jumps. An invert looks showier, but I think spinning is actually harder. It's so easy to catch an edge and bounce the landing.

I liked the height of the jump, so I decided on a spin. I went off on my front foot to help it, hopping up instead of gliding off. I was already in the air by the time my back foot was at the edge. That gave me a little extra time. I spun and landed clean.

Next was a rail. I leaned over and floated down, barely touching the rail. I had to turn pretty sharply to reach the next jump, but I did, and made it an invert this time. I spread out to stall the jump when I was upside down, then curled up again to continue the rotation. That should be worth extra points.

I had played it safe so far, counting on style to get me a good score, but if I wanted to win, I needed to take a risk. I went high on an embankment and did another spin off the top before coming down like it was a half-pipe. There was another choice coming up: tabletop or big jump. All the serious competitors so far had hit the big jump. I needed to do that too, and make it count.

I'd managed to pull off the backside rodeo when Ted was watching. I didn't pull it off every time though, despite what I'd told him.

I crouched low to pick up speed and started into my spin before I was even all the way off the lip of the jump. It was too soon. My spin carried me too far around, and I had to change my flip to a simple grab or risk bailing.

Later, I waited by the judges' booth with the other competitors. We milled around, trying not to look anxious as we listened to the announcer thanking the sponsors and the hill and everyone short of his pet hamster. Trying to look cool.

Finally, he came to it. Third place went to some guy I didn't know. I slid my back teeth against each other, shifting my jaw around. Why do they start from the bottom? Why not just announce first place first, so everyone could relax?

"And in second place," the announcer said, "Jamie Clark."

We were looking at each other as he said it. She grinned, then frowned, then grinned again, almost faster than I could follow. She seemed to settle on being happy as she went to get her prize. She shook hands with the announcer, who held on longer than I thought was necessary. On her way back to the crowd, she caught my eye and mouthed, "Congratulations."

She figured that if she hadn't won, I had. I wasn't sure. My hands were sweaty. There was that last jump I had blown.

And Ted had phoned Jamie, not me. Didn't that mean she was the better rider?

"The winner of this year's Burton Slopestyle Competition is...," he said, drawing it out for effect, "...Ryan Sullivan."

Five hundred dollars. Five hundred dollars and a new board, and, best of all, the chance to meet with the Burton people and talk about sponsorship. There was even going to be an article in *Boarder* magazine. Not about me, but about the event. Maybe they would mention me by name.

I couldn't keep the big, stupid grin off my face. I probably looked stoned. I didn't even care, I was that happy.

This was it. The first step on my way to becoming a professional boarder. I wished my parents were here. They'd phoned in the morning to wish me luck, but it wasn't the same.

Someone punched me in the shoulder. "Yo. That's you, right? Ryan? You're supposed to be up there."

Right. Not a good time to space out. "Thanks," I said as I headed up to the microphone.

I took my gloves off to shake the announcer's hand properly. A guy in a Burton polar fleece sweater stood beside him, smiling. He shook my hand too. "Congratulations, Ryan," he said. "I look forward to speaking with you after the ceremony."

I'm pretty sure I was in goofy grin territory by then, because he sort of laughed, then turned me back to the crowd. "Ryan Sullivan," he said. People clapped.

My cell phone rang. Clapping turned to laughter. "He's in demand already," the Burton guy said. My face got hot. I fumbled for the phone's Off switch, but when I looked at the display, I saw Kevin's number. He must have heard that I won. I grinned, grateful that he had bothered to call. It was a good way to end the silent treatment. There were a lot of people in that tent, but not one of them was there just for me. Kevin's phone call kind of made up for that.

By now the announcer had moved onto something else, and no one was paying attention to me anymore. I flipped open the phone. "Hey, Kev," I said.

"Ryan? Thank god, man. I wasn't sure you were gonna answer." That wasn't a "Congratulations" voice. That was a panicked voice.

"What's wrong?"

"I need you to meet me at the lift hut. Now. On the east side."

"I'm right in the middle of the Burton thing," I said. "I can't leave now. I have to talk to them about a sponsorship. There's a reporter here too." I was a little hurt that Kevin hadn't remembered the competition.

"Cuz." It was nearly a whine. "I wouldn't ask if it wasn't important."

He had me there. It was true. He wouldn't have called me unless something was seriously wrong. "I'll be right there," I promised.

chapter ten

I peeled away from the crowd and grabbed my board from the competitors' area. Jamie gave me a funny look, but there was no time to explain. Kevin could be a prickly pain in the butt, and I was pretty sure he was mixed up in some shady dealings, but he was still my cousin. If he needed help, I was there. He'd have done the same for me. I think.

There was no way to get directly to where Kevin was from where I was. I had to head down a short hill, then take a chair-lift and go down another run. Longest lift ride of my life. I swung my left leg back and forth in the air (my board was strapped to my right leg, or I'd have swung both) and growled every time the lift paused.

As soon as my chair neared the top, where there was about a ten-foot drop to the ground, I jumped off.

I landed on my hands and knees in the snow and rolled over to fasten on my board. I think all of twelve seconds passed between the time I jumped and the time I started boarding down the hill. I resented every one of them.

The hill was an easy ride, and I made good time down to the lift hut. As I approached, I saw Kevin leaning against the wall. There was a short line of people waiting for the lift, but another lift attendant was helping them. Maybe Kevin had gotten someone to cover for him when... whatever it was that had freaked him out had happened.

As I got closer, I changed my mind. He didn't look panicked. He looked relaxed.

I scraped snow to stop in front of him. "What's wrong?" I asked.

He flashed me a smile that was almost sheepish. "Sorry, cuz. Crisis averted. Thanks for coming though. It means a lot."

I think I popped a blood vessel in my eye, because things very literally looked red for a second. "No freakin' way. You didn't call me down here to tell me that nothing's the matter." I leaned on my toe edge, placing one arm on either side of Kevin. Not sure what I was trying to do. Trap him there?

He shoved me, hard enough that I slid back on my board and almost caught my heel edge. I hopped, regaining my balance.

"Or what?" he asked.

At that moment I hated him.

"Or nothing," I said. My voice was too loud. Some of the people in the lift line were staring, but I didn't care. "Just that I left the freakin' Burton competition to come find you. Which I won, by the way, thanks for asking. Just that I'm supposed to be talking about a sponsorship deal right now, and I've probably pissed off a whole lot of important people, taking off like that to get down here for whatever emergency you were supposedly having. Screw you."

He stuffed his hands in his pocket. "I didn't know," he said.

"'Course not," I said. "Tell me what's going on." I moved to the side, using my body to screen us from view as much as I could.

"Can't," he said. He sighed, like I was making a really big deal out of nothing. "Look, something went down, and I kind of freaked, so I called you. Sorry. But I figured out...what I needed to do, so things are fine." I was pretty sure he'd changed his mind about what he was going to say. I'd have loved to know what he stopped himself from saying.

"I'm glad you called me." I met his eyes straight on, so he'd know I meant it.

His mouth worked a bit, but he didn't say anything. "I am," I continued finally. "I'm glad you think you can do that if things go wrong. But if you're not going to tell me the truth, don't bother calling me again."

He let me past the lineup to get on the lift. One of the other lifties started to say something, but Kevin glared at him. He didn't let anyone else on my chair either, which was good. I wasn't in the mood to deal with anyone. Kevin got the chair for me, and he didn't slam it into the back of my knees, like he normally would have done. Not that I like being smacked by a big hunk of metal, but it made me feel weird, how careful he was being. We didn't act like that with each other.

Getting back to the Burton tent was the same as getting down to Kevin. There was no direct route. I rode the lift up, boarded down a short hill, and got on another lift to carry me to the top of the slopestyle run. The competition was over. The run was open to the public again. I rode down, taking my time, hitting that jump I had screwed up during the comp.

People were still milling around the Burton tent at the bottom of the run, but there weren't nearly as many of them as there had been before. A woman I recognized from the main office stopped me. "Where did you disappear to? The Burton people wanted to talk to you. We needed you for the photo shoot too."

"There was something I had to do," I said. "Family emergency."

She frowned. I could tell she didn't believe me. What kind of a family emergency means you have to ride away on a snowboard, and then show up again forty minutes later?

"Your prize is in the office," she said, still frowning.

I nodded. "Where are the Burton people now?"

"Gone," she said. "They couldn't wait around forever, nor could the reporters.

Luckily, the second place winner was available to take your place for the interview and the photos."

Jamie? Jamie had taken my place for the *Boarder* magazine article?

I caught her eye across the tent. She waved, and her mouth made the shape of my name, but I turned around. My big shot, and I'd screwed it up. Not only that, but Jamie had taken my place.

"Ryan!"

I pretended I didn't hear her.

I felt weirdly numb as I walked out of the tent, which might have been why all the activity didn't register right away. There were five police cars parked outside the main lodge, lights flashing. I'd have walked right past them, except that as I approached the door, two policemen came out with Archie, the lift supervisor.

I grabbed the first person I saw who was wearing a hill uniform. A ski instructor, it turned out. "What is this?"

"Drug bust, I heard," she said. "Crazy, eh?"

Crazy. Yeah. Just like everything else about this day.

Later, on the way home, I talked to Kevin. Tried to, anyhow. Yeah, after all that had happened, we had started sharing a ride again. Not much choice. I had to give him credit for not ditching me at the ski hill, no matter how mad we were at each other.

"Did you hear about it? Is that what had you freaked out?" I was still trying to fit the pieces together, trying to sort out what the police had to do with the white van and the stolen ski equipment. Maybe that was it...maybe they had nothing to do with it, but when Kevin heard there were police at the hill, he panicked. By the time I got to him, he'd learned about the drug bust, so he knew he wasn't in trouble.

"How would I hear about something like that, all the way out in the lift hut?" he asked. "Besides, I thought you said the police weren't there until after."

I pressed harder, but he didn't give me anything new. It wasn't until way later that night, while I was doing some·research online, that I realized he hadn't actually answered my question.

Didn't matter. I smiled at the screen in front of me. Turned out a person could find a lot of things online. Even instructions for breaking into a car.

chapter eleven

I think Kevin was shocked by how easygoing I became over the next couple of days. I didn't ask him any questions, didn't blow up at him for avoiding me, didn't do anything to show that something was wrong. He acted weird at first, like he didn't know how to take me, but after the first day or so he relaxed. It was probably good luck that I ended up with some extra shifts at the gas station. It took up a lot of my time after school. I'd rather have been boarding, but the extra money was good, and time away from Kevin was a bonus.

I hated being in the same room as Kevin and feeling like a stranger. Neither of us has any brothers or sisters, and we'd grown up together. This—whatever it was—felt wrong.

On our third day back at the ski hill after the competition, I saw the white van again. It wasn't white anymore though. It had been painted gray, but I was pretty sure it was the same van. I compared the license plate with the picture on my cell phone to make sure.

After school on a weeknight, the hill tends to be busy with school groups. A lot of these kids have never been on a board (or skis) before, and some of them try to keep up with their friends who have. It's usually busy in the patrol hut. At five o'clock the school busses leave, and the hill gets a lot quieter.

After five, I found a sheltered corner on the outside of the ski lodge to hang out in. It was kind of cold, but at least the building cut the wind. I could see the parking lot, but it was dark enough that no one would see me unless they looked right at me. I watched.

It took so long that I started to doubt myself. Maybe I was wrong. Maybe there was nothing going on. I was almost ready to give up when I saw a kid in snowboard boots carry a pair of skis out to the van.

I stayed in my corner, even after the kid left. I wondered how many people were in on the theft, and if they each had a key to the van. Did Kevin? The day I had watched him, there had been someone waiting in the back of the van. His "friend" with the big jaw and the ugly beard. Because of the way the parking lot was set up, I hadn't been able to see what the kid did with the skis, only that he carried them to the van and then left without them.

I had done my online research. I wouldn't need a key to get into that van. I just had to be sure there was no one inside. I waited, figuring everyone needs a nature break sometime, right?

After another ten or fifteen minutes, a guy left the van. The guy with the stupid beard and the sticking-out jaw.

Jaws (as I decided to call him) walked right past me on his way into the lodge. He either didn't see me leaning against the wall or decided that some random snowboard punk was not worth his notice. As soon as he entered the building, I moved.

The instructions that I had found online were supposed to work for older model cars. The van looked pretty old—cassette player-and-manual-locks kind of old. Of course, I'd never broken into anything before, so I was taking a lot on faith.

I had packed my "tools" days ago. In my jacket pocket were a butter knife (the instructions said to use a putty knife, but I didn't have one of those), the doorstop from Kevin's room and a bent coat hanger. I had straightened it, but then I'd rolled it up loosely to make it fit into my pocket. I had wrapped an elastic band around one end of the hanger, where the last inch or so was bent at ninety degrees, to make a grippy bit for the lock button.

Yup, I was ready to go pro.

I moved to the passenger side of the van, since it was less visible from the building. The last thing I needed was to get caught. I reached up and slid my knife into the crack between the door and the roof of the van.

I kind of twisted the knife and got a little opening, then tried to jam the door-stop in there. It wouldn't go. I worked the knife around a bit. Still no luck. Damn.

The blade of the knife was wedged into the car, but I didn't have the leverage to make a big enough opening for the door-stop. It had looked really easy when the guy online did it. Then again, he'd been in a nice, sunny driveway, working on a Corolla. I was in a slippery, snow-covered parking lot, freezing my fingers off while I tried to jimmy a wedge into an opening that was too high for me to see.

It wasn't going to work. I yanked on the knife one more time for good measure, using all my body weight. The handle broke off. Stupid, cheap piece of cutlery. I threw the broken handle. It skated away over the hard-packed snow. I thought about throwing the door wedge but shoved it back in my pocket instead.

I glared at the lock button. Nasty surprise number two: my trick wouldn't have worked anyway. The lock button wasn't the kind with a wide top like a golf tee. It was the kind with a skinny, tapered top. There would have been nothing for me to grab onto. Guess I should have checked before I started in with the butter knife and the door wedge.

That was when I realized I was seeing an awful lot of that lock button.

No. No freaking way.

I tried the door. It was unlocked.

Yes, I was officially the world's worst car thief.

I opened the door and climbed in. The first thing I noticed was the smell, kind of sweet. It smelled like someone had been smoking up in there. I knew that smell well enough. I'd tried it a couple of times a few years ago, but it's not my scene. Some of the older pro boarders are so used to smoking up before they ride that they're no good without it; I never want to be that guy. Besides, a lot of the big competitions have random drug testing.

I scrambled between the front seats to get to the back, where I'd be less visible. The van was open behind the bench seat, creating a nice, big storage area. Just what every petty crook needs. When I looked over the back of the seat, I whistled. They had the beginnings of a good ski swap in there, and this was probably only one day's work.

Skis and boards were stacked in neat piles. Some were wrapped in blankets. I figured those were the expensive ones. There were blue gym bags back there too, packed full of something. I took a couple of pictures with my phone.

I climbed over the back of the seat to crouch beside one of the gym bags.

The smell was stronger back here. I unzipped the bag. Inside was package after package of tightly compressed leaves. I sniffed one to be sure, but I was already feeling a bit nauseous.

There was enough weed in that one bag to cover my college tuition next year. Maybe with some left over. I'm no expert on the going prices, but the tourists here have cash. I was pretty sure Jaws and his buddies made at least as much money out of the blue gym bags as they did stealing equipment—probably way more. It didn't make any sense to me, why they would do both. It wasn't like I could ask Kevin either.

I snapped a few more pictures. It was dark inside the van, so the pictures probably wouldn't turn out great, but it was the best I could do.

I climbed over the bench seat again, planning to go out the way I had come in, and I froze. Through the front window, I saw Jaws walking back to the van.

chapter twelve

I stared at Jaws through the front window of the van. My throat made a weird, croaking sound.

Okay. Plan B. I hadn't seen him using the front doors, so I figured he'd come in the back way. Back door or side door? I waited, crouched down, until he passed the front windows. My hands shook a little, like before the competition. I counted to three and scrambled between the front seats.

The instant I heard the back door open, I burst out through the passenger door.

"Hey!" Jaws had heard me, but I was already running. Behind me, I heard footsteps. I didn't look back.

I ran toward the ski lodge, dodging around the parked cars. At least that way, if he caught me, there would be people around.

I didn't bother to run hunched over. He had already seen me, and I didn't have much chance of losing him by hiding behind a car. I just tried for speed. Should have watched my step though. I skidded on an icy patch and nearly fell. I grabbed whatever was closest and ended up half-sprawled over the trunk of a Jetta. Jaws was coming around the other side. I stood so the car was between us; then we played the dodge-left, dodge-right game. He had a nasty grin. The kind where you can picture the teeth being used to gnaw bones or raw flesh.

Finally, I broke away. I was closer to the lodge, but Jaws wasn't far behind.

I spotted a ski instructor, her kindergarten-age class trailing behind her, holding onto a rope as they penguin-walked to the baby hill. Perfect. I put on a burst of speed and zoomed past. Jaws would have to go around the kids. That bought me a few seconds.

I pushed my way through a crowd of teenagers. They weren't happy, but that was only going to make it tougher for Jaws to get through. Finally, I was in the lodge. There's a small room with a door that's not even labeled. It's the volunteer locker room. I've got a locker in there, but I hardly ever bother to use it. Going in was a risk. If he followed me, I'd be trapped in a small room with him. If he was as far behind as I thought, I'd have a good hiding place. I stomped the snow and ice off my boots as best I could on the carpets, so I wouldn't leave a trail.

I made it into the room. It was empty. Dark green lockers lined the walls, most of them locked, some not. There was a wooden bench in the middle of the room. That was about it. No hiding places. Unless...

I opened one of the lockers that didn't have a padlock on it. There was a jacket in there and a pair of boots. Somebody was trusting. There wasn't even anything important in my locker, just some ratty old spare clothes, and I still kept a lock on it— which was why I wasn't going to be able hide in my own locker now. No time to undo a lock.

I squeezed myself into the open locker. I'm not exactly locker-sized, and the jacket and boots didn't help. A fair bit of ducking over and hunching my shoulders was involved. I managed to pull the door closed with my fingertips.

Just in time. The door to the locker room opened.

I couldn't see. All I could do was hold my breath and wait. I counted to ten in my head before the door closed again. There was no other sound. It didn't seem like anyone had come into the room to use a locker. Jaws had been looking for me.

I stayed in that locker for a long time.

chapter thirteen

I needed to talk to Kevin. The people he was involved with had seen me. Jaws had chased me. I needed to know exactly how much trouble I was in.

I was also thinking it might be time to go to the police, but I wanted to give my cousin a heads-up. I wasn't sure what he would do, but I owed him something. He'd told me to stay away. I hadn't listened.

Besides, when had the police ever done my family any favors? Dad's "anonymous tip" about his company's pollution had landed him in Winnipeg.

I looked for Kevin on the hill and tried his cell phone. No luck. I wasn't worried though. After school today, he had driven me to the hill in his truck. He'd drive me back to his parents' place tonight. I'd talk to him then.

Sweep was over, the hill was closed. I waited by Kevin's truck. He was due any minute. There was no sign of Jaws's van in the parking lot, thank god.

Ten minutes later I was still waiting, leaning against the cab, getting colder by the second. Somehow I didn't think it was a good idea to put my newfound lock-picking skills to use. Especially since I had no lock-picking skills.

Nope, no Kevin. Instead, I saw the one person (besides Jaws) I least wanted to see. Jamie. She was carrying her board, probably about to leave for the night, when she spotted me and changed direction.

We hadn't talked, but she had to have figured out by now that I was pissed off.

Whenever I saw her on the hill, I took off in the other direction. If she didn't know why...well, it wasn't my problem.

Besides, it didn't take a rocket scientist to figure out that if you steal a guy's magazine interview, he's not going to be happy.

She stood in front of me, looking kind of awkward. I had never seen Jamie look awkward before.

"Hey," she said. Then she stopped, like she wasn't sure what else to say.

"How's it going?" I said. I hoped my tone of voice told her that I didn't really care. For once, I seemed to have more words than Jamie.

"Are you mad? About the magazine thing?"

I shrugged. "No big deal."

"I wouldn't have done it, but they were in a hurry, and no one could find you. Where did you go, anyhow? Didn't you hear them paging you?"

Okay, so Jamie still had more words than I did. "Don't worry about it," I said.

In a flash she went from awkward to angry. "Well, I wouldn't, except that you're all of a sudden acting like a big freaking jerk! What's with you, anyhow? You were the one who left. Just like you showed up late for Ted. I thought you were different from those other losers. I thought you were serious."

I met her eyes. "I am serious," I said. And I was. She didn't understand.

"Then what's wrong with you? You're blowing every chance you get."

That was a bit rich, coming from the girl who had benefited each time I screwed up. "What do you care?"

She stepped back. "I don't."

She turned and made a gesture that might have been a wave or a flip of her hand. And then I was alone again. Great. Good for me.

My cell phone vibrated in my pocket. I pulled it out. A text message from Kevin.

Gone to a friend's. Go home without me.

That was it? No explanation, no apology, nothing? And since when did Kevin text? He always phoned.

Go home without me. Yeah, like it was so easy—even if I had a key to his truck, which I didn't. I turned seventeen last December, but I still hadn't gotten my full driver's license yet.

Crap. I kicked the tire. What was I supposed to do now? Walk for an hour in the freezing cold? Call my aunt and uncle for a ride? Kevin didn't even care. Leave me stranded, inconvenience his parents... he didn't give a damn.

Headlights flashed over the truck. I heard tires crunching on snow. A VW Golf pulled up in front of me. I was completely unsurprised to see Jamie at the wheel. It made sense, didn't it? I was stranded, humiliated and kicking tires. Of course she would see it.

She rolled down the window. "What's wrong?"

I shook my head. "It's fine."

"Do you need a ride?"

If she had asked like she felt sorry for me, I'd have said no and walked home. She didn't. She just asked it straight out. Did I need a ride, like did I want fries with that. Somehow that made it easier to say yes.

She popped the trunk so I could lay my board on top of hers, and then I got into the car. It had this lemony smell from an air freshener clipped to the air vent. "Thanks," I said.

"Don't mention it." We got all the way out of the parking lot and onto the concession road before she spoke again. "So what's going on with you?"

I groaned.

She shrugged. "No such thing as a free ride. You've got a cell phone. I could let you out right here and not even feel guilty. Much."

I didn't believe her. It was pitch-black and unpopulated out here. Not that I'm afraid of the dark. I just couldn't picture

Jamie abandoning someone by the side of the road.

Still. She was being nice, and maybe she deserved some kind of explanation. Besides, who else did I have to talk to?

"There's just some stuff going on with my cousin," I said. "He's been acting weird. I think maybe he's involved in something he shouldn't be."

She laughed. "That's exactly what I told my friends about you."

She had told her friends about me? I tried to act like my ears hadn't just perked up. "Nothing going on with me. Except, you know, by extension." I told her about my board being stolen and Kevin returning it. I told her about his panicky phone call right after the competition, and how, when I got down there, nothing was wrong. And about how he stood me up, which was why I needed the lift home. I didn't tell her about the van or about being chased.

She was a good listener. Didn't say much, just nodded sometimes. I felt better for telling at least some of the story to someone.

There was a weird moment when she pulled up outside my aunt and uncle's house. "So, uh, I'll see you," she said.

I unfastened my seat belt. "Yeah. Thanks. For the ride and all."

"Can I see your phone?"

I thought that was weird, but I handed it to her. She punched a number in. "There. Now you can call me if you ever need to talk. I won't tell anyone."

"Thanks." I took the phone back from her. We sat there for a few seconds in the dark car. It felt like that moment at the end of a first date, when you're not sure whether to kiss and you're trying to read the vibe from the girl. Only this wasn't a date. It wasn't anything like that. I opened the door. "Drive safe, okay?"

"Yeah. Good night," she said. She popped the trunk so I could get my board.

I watched until she drove away, and then I went inside.

My aunt and uncle were both on the couch in the family room, watching TV, but he was dozing. "I thought you might call for a ride," she said when she saw me. "Kevin phoned us to say something came up."

I paused in the doorway. "He phoned?"

"Yes. He wanted to make sure we were going to be home if you needed us." She paused. "Didn't he tell you?"

"I guess I forgot," I said. "Did he sound okay?"

"Why wouldn't he?"

"No reason."

She sighed. "Ryan, I do know when my son has been drinking. It's all right, so long as he tells me where he is and he's not driving. I won't pretend to like it, but I appreciate his phoning. Is there something else you're worried about?"

I shook my head. "No. Just checking."

"Oh, I almost forgot. There was a message for you. A Ted Travis? He left his number. I wrote it down on the pad by the phone. Your parents called too." She eyed me.

It had been a while since I had spoken to them. But with the time difference, that would have to wait for another night.

"Ted called?" I ran to the kitchen.

Five minutes later, I should have been the happiest boarder in BC. He wanted me in the shoot. It was going to be slopestyle, like Jamie said, done on the back forty. It was going to be great.

I should have been thrilled, but something didn't feel right. It was great about the video shoot, but without someone to share the news with—someone who would actually get what it meant—it wasn't the same. If Kevin had been there, and if things were normal between us, I'd have told him. I felt unsettled as I headed to my room. Kevin's room, really, but he wasn't in the other bed.

There was someone I could tell though. Someone who would get it.

I sat on my bed and dialed Jamie's number.

chapter fourteen

Kevin didn't come home that night. After school the next day, my aunt drove me to the ski hill, even though Kevin was working. I was only on for a couple of hours anyhow—until six.

It was a busy day. Lots of schoolkids on the slopes. The snow had softened during the day, then was slick and fast again by late afternoon. There had been two little snowboarders in the patrol hut when I first got there, both with broken wrists. The calls kept coming after that.

Late in the shift, Allison got me to reload a toboggan that had been used for an earlier patient. Splints on the bottom, then backboard, then the gym bag containing all the straps and collars. I strapped the waterproof cover in place and headed into the hut to see if she needed anything else. I was itching to get back onto the hill.

"Can you take the toboggan up to the cache, Ryan?" she asked, looking up from the patient she was treating—a schoolkid with a bloody nose. There were toboggan caches all over the hill—long wooden boxes with padlocked doors. The toboggans were stored there so it was easy to get at them when they were needed.

I had only taken one up the hill, in training. "I think so," I said.

"Good." She shoved a bit of hair out of her face with her forearm. She was wearing rubber gloves. "We need them all up there today, and I don't have any patrollers free."

A toboggan with just equipment on it isn't that heavy. Its size is the real problem. It's not easy to haul an eight-foot-long plastic sled up on a chairlift and balance it there. Doable, but awkward.

I boarded down to the center chairlift, the closest one to the hut, toboggan in tow. Luckily, I didn't have to wait in line when I was bringing a toboggan up. It would have been a pain trying to manhandle it through the lift lines.

When I got to the lift, I wished Allison had picked somebody else for the job. Kevin was loading a family of skiers onto the chair. He hadn't seen me yet.

There were two little kids with their parents, so he didn't slam the lift or anything. He slowed it right down and made sure they were all okay before he turned up the speed again. And he asked the little boy if he thought the mom was ready, instead of the other way around. It was such a Kevin thing to do that, for a second, I forgot how messed up everything was.

Then he saw me. He'd been smiling a bit, but when he saw me, his face went blank.

"Can I bring this up?" I asked.

"Sure." I might as well have been a stranger, the way he said it. He loaded one more chair and then stopped the lift. I dragged the toboggan out, and he brought a chair up really slowly. He even lifted the back of the toboggan and helped me get it balanced across the seat, but he didn't say a word, even when I thanked him.

Then I was headed up the hill, and Kevin was on the ground behind me. That was that.

By the time I had wrestled the toboggan into the cache, my shift was nearly over. I decided to take the most direct route back to the patrol hut, even if it wasn't one of my favorite runs. The sooner I got rid of my radio, the sooner I could head to the back of the hill to practice for Ted's video. I hadn't done a lot of off-trail riding lately. It was one of those things that wasn't technically allowed, but happened anyhow.

I was halfway down the run when I saw the accident. A little girl was snowplowing and crossing the whole width of the hill. She didn't belong on an intermediate run. The guy on a board behind her knew what he was doing, but he was going way too fast. He came over a rise in the hill and even got a little air, but didn't look where he was going.

I don't think she even saw him. One minute she was skiing, the next she was flying. The guy fell too, but full-grown man versus sixty-pound girl is really no contest.

It was a yard sale—the patrol term for a messy accident, with skis and poles everywhere. By the time I got to them, he was sitting up. She wasn't.

"Oh, jeez," he said. "Oh, man."

I ignored him. I jammed my board in the snow just uphill from the little girl, so people would know to go around; then I knelt down beside her. "Can you hear me? Uh, don't move, but can you open your eyes?"

She did, turning her head a bit to look at me.

"No, don't do that," I said. I put my right hand on her forehead—she didn't even have a helmet on. "This is just to remind you not to move, okay?" With my left hand, I fumbled for my radio and called Allison.

The little girl watched me. She had big brown eyes, like a puppy dog. She didn't say anything.

"Do you hurt anywhere?" I asked.

"My leg."

I looked down. Her left leg stuck out at kind of a weird angle. It sort of rolled sideways from her body, and it looked a bit shorter than her right. I knew that wasn't good.

"Okay," I said. "There will be someone here to help you really soon, all right?"

"Okay," she echoed. She seemed way too calm. Almost tired. Her breathing seemed kind of fast and shallow, like a bird's. I knew that wasn't good either. That meant shock.

The man who hit her had walked over. "Oh, god," he said. "I'm so sorry." He looked like he was going to start crying any second.

"You want to help?" I asked.

He nodded.

"Give her your jacket," I said. I couldn't take mine off without letting go of her head, and I didn't want to do that.

He seemed happy to do something useful. He spread his coat over her.

"Now stand up there by my snowboard," I said. "Make sure no one comes too close. And when you see the patrol coming, wave them over here."

I know it couldn't have been long before the patrollers showed, but it felt like forever. I found out the little girl's name was Katy, and I talked to her about all kinds of things. Anything I could think of. I just wanted to keep her awake and make her eyes stop sliding out of focus. It worked, some of the time.

The patrollers were gentle with her, but I could tell it still hurt. She screamed when they splinted her leg, but at least then it was straight again and not shortened. Once they had her on the backboard, they didn't need to move her anymore. That was better, I thought.

Until they loaded her into the toboggan. She freaked out. If she hadn't been strapped down, she probably would have hurt herself. I didn't blame her, really. It must have been scary, being unable to move like that. By then, Allison had arrived, and she knelt down beside Katy, talking to her. Finally, she stood and walked over to me.

"She wants you to go down with her," Allison said. "Ride where she can see you. We've got a snowmobile coming to meet us at the bottom of the hill for the ride up to the patrol hut." The hut was several hills over and an uphill climb from the bottom of the hill we were on. Snowmobile was standard procedure. "You'll be on the back of the snowmobile, facing backward. Watch her. If she raises an arm, it means something's wrong, so you get the driver to stop. Can you do that, Ryan?"

I nodded. There was no time for more questions. Allison wanted to get Katy off the hill and into an ambulance, fast.

The first part was easy. Allison stepped into the toboggan's handlebars to ski in front, while another patroller wrapped a rope around his waist and boarded down behind the toboggan, keeping the rope taut. I did what I was told and stayed beside the toboggan, where Katy could see me.

We reached the bottom of the hill okay. There was a crowd waiting. Allison yelled at them to move out of the way. If that hadn't done the trick, the roar of the snowmobile would have.

Allison hooked the toboggan to the back and motioned for me to get on the seat behind the driver. I did.

Allison picked up my board. "See you at the hut," she said.

The snowmobile lurched forward. Katy's hand flew up. I reached behind me to tap the driver. "She wants to stop," I yelled.

I jumped off as soon as he stopped and ran over to Katy. "What's wrong?" I asked.

"I'm scared."

Me too, kid, I thought. She looked worse than before. Paler.

"You have to be brave, okay? We need to get you to the hut so we can look after you properly. Just think of it as a fun ride."

Her lip trembled. "I want Mommy."

I wanted her mommy to be there too, because Katy shouldn't be stuck with just me for moral support. "I know. We'll find her once we get to the hut, okay?" I wished I had a teddy bear or something to give her. "Want my scarf? You can hold onto it." It was the only soft thing I had.

Kevin used to bug me about it. It's got a snowflake pattern, and there's this giant tassel on each end.

It was a weird idea, I know, but she seemed to think it was funny. "Okay," she said. So I gave it to her, and she grabbed it like it really was a bear or something, and we made it the rest of the way to the patrol hut.

Things happened fast after that. The ambulance was already waiting, so they loaded Katy right in. Someone had found her parents, I don't know how. If you asked me, she was a bit young to be skiing without them in the first place, but I saw it all the time. Maybe she had gone off with some friends and gotten into trouble. I didn't ask; I didn't want her parents to feel like I was questioning them or something. After all, I was hardly the poster boy for slope safety.

After the ambulance left, I realized Katy was still holding onto my scarf. That made me feel kind of good. I figured she needed it more than I did. I hoped it helped.

chapter fifteen

It took me a while to find my board, which gave me a disturbing sense of déjà vu. I finally found it jumbled in with a bunch of other stuff outside the patrol hut, right where Allison had said it was. I was sure I'd already looked there, but I must have been distracted.

My shift was over. I was glad. I didn't want to deal with anything else today. As I rode the lift, I kept thinking about Katy and how scared she had been.

I needed to be moving. Once I was riding, I wouldn't think so much.

By the time I reached the top of the mountain, the sky was overcast and the light was getting flat. I wasn't sure I'd get a better opportunity though. I wanted to practice on the back forty by myself, before Ted's video shoot. We were due for snow. He wanted fresh powder for the shoot, so we were doing it tomorrow.

There was no way I was making a fool of myself again. I wasn't sure why he had changed his mind, or why he had waited so long to call me, but I wanted to make the most of my second chance.

Only the most advanced riders bothered with the lift that runs to the top of the mountain. Of those, not all had a taste for out-of-bounds skiing or boarding, and this wasn't exactly the time of day for it. I didn't expect to run into anyone. That was fine with me.

I got off the lift and started the long hike off the groomed area of the ski hill, keeping one eye on the sky. I had time to get a decent run in and make it back to groomed territory before nightfall. The starting point I had in mind meant a brief run through trees, leading into the more open area where Ted wanted to shoot.

It might have been because I was in such a hurry that I didn't pay as much attention as I should have. I was in the trees and three turns down before I noticed that something was wrong. My bindings were loose on the board. They rattled when I turned.

I struggled for control, but I was going too fast. My board shot free. It hurtled down the hill without me. I hit the snow hard and flipped, my bindings still attached to my boots. It hurt.

I tucked and rolled. I was still in the trees. Bad place to fall.

I don't know if I was just stunned from the fall or what, but it took a while for me to notice that I had stopped moving. My head was angled back, resting on my helmet.

I looked up through tree branches at a darkening sky. My body felt heavy.

I tried to roll over. Nothing happened. My legs didn't want to move. I didn't hurt anywhere. I just felt like something was holding me down. My brain worked slowly. I realized I wasn't lying on top of the snow, I was buried in it. My feet were down below my head, not quite like I was standing upright, but almost. I lifted my right arm out of soft, fluffy snow. My left was pinned against my side. I tried to pull it out, but more snow tumbled in, and suddenly I was buried up to my neck. I stopped moving.

I was in a tree well.

All of a sudden, my chest felt tight, like I couldn't breathe. No one knew where I was. No one was going to come looking for me. I had to get myself out. I thrashed, trying to swim through the snow, trying to reach a tree or more solid ground or anything that would help me haul myself out of there.

It was no good. All my thrashing only sunk me a couple of inches lower. I needed to stay still, stay calm. It was getting dark. In a couple of hours, the patrol would do a sweep. If I was lucky, someone might notice my tracks going off from the top of the hill. Maybe they would investigate.

Maybe Kevin would notice if I wasn't at his truck. We hadn't talked about him driving me home today, but I figured he'd let me know, at least. If he called and I didn't pick up...he would just assume I was still pissed off. He wouldn't tell anyone.

My aunt would know something was wrong when I didn't come home. How late would it be before she got worried?

It was darker here, in the trees. I was already getting cold.

My cell phone, tucked into my pocket, vibrated. A text message. Kevin, probably. I laughed at the uselessness of having a phone in my pocket when I couldn't move my arm to reach it. It wasn't normal, healthy laughter—more the hysterical kind. Still, it was a noise in the darkness, and I decided I liked it. Like the night when I had gone looking for that guy in the woods. Better my voice than no voice.

So I talked. I did an audio commentary for Ted's video. "And now we have Jamie with a perfect three-sixty off the cliff... these sorts of rotations are actually harder than the flips, since it's difficult to judge the landing, but she pulls it off. Ryan's right behind her, and—did you see that, folks? Nice backside rodeo. Beautiful. Let's play that again."

Okay, it wasn't a very good commentary.

When I got bored with it, I talked to Kevin. Told him what a dick he was being, and how worried I was that he was in over his head. My dad never talked about it much, but I knew he was lucky to get out alive when the plant had to close. He did the right thing, going to the police about the toxins, but the company owners had decided it was easier to close the plant than to clean up the mess. A lot of guys were angry when they lost their jobs—*really* angry, which was why my parents had left town. So I knew what it looked like when someone was in over his head, but at least my dad had had a reason for taking the risk. Kevin was just being stupid.

Suddenly I really, really missed my dad. I felt like I needed to talk to him. He didn't even know I was proud of him.

Tears. Great. They'd freeze. I blinked them away. But I still felt the stinging wetness on my face, and that was when I realized it was snowing.

Snow was bad. Snow would cover my tracks.

If we got enough of it, I'd suffocate.

chapter sixteen

The snow piled higher. It was cold. I was getting tired. I knew that wasn't a good thing.

I knew this mountain inside out. The real problem, my real mistake, had been not checking my board. I should have realized the binding screws were loose.

But how had they gotten loose? I'd been riding right before that, when I came across Katy. My board had been fine then.

But Allison had taken it. Maybe given it to somebody. I had no idea. What I did know was that my board had been unattended for I didn't know how long while we got Katy loaded into the ambulance and took care of the paperwork. If someone had wanted to mess with it, that would have been a good time.

Suddenly I felt even colder. Someone had done this to me on purpose? Sure, I'd done it to other riders when I was younger. My friends and I used to do it as a joke, but only when we were riding somewhere safe. It was stupid. I knew that. It was stupid anytime, to send a board shooting down a hill out of control, but...well, we did it.

I closed my eyes. Snowflakes matted my eyelashes. I still had my right arm free. I wiped my face clear. I'd be able to keep the snow from piling up around my face for a while.

Someone who knew what my board looked like had done this to me. I could have died from the fall. Dying was still a strong possibility.

I decided not to think about that part too much. Someone would find me. Somebody had to find me. Maybe even the joker who had pulled this stunt.

But they couldn't have known where I was going. If I'd just done a normal run, the loose board wouldn't have been a problem. Probably. Depending on when it decided to work loose.

"It's a warning." As I said the words, I knew they were true. Someone wanted me to know they could get to me. Jaws? Or maybe somebody who worked for him. But Kevin was the only one who knew for sure what my board looked like.

I very much wanted it not to have been Kevin. Jaws, maybe. He was a shark, anyhow.

It was getting hard to think.

In my pocket, my phone buzzed again. "Sorry, nobody home," I whispered.

I couldn't be bothered to open my eyes. There didn't seem to be much point. It was all darkness, anyhow. Darkness and falling snow.

I was still shivering. That was a good sign.

Then I heard a voice. Probably not a good sign, hearing voices. "If you're my guardian angel, you suck," I said.

"Ryan?"

It was Jamie's voice. Jamie was my guardian angel? That didn't make sense. "Nobody home," I said. I started laughing again.

"Over here!" Then Jamie was lying flat on her board, reaching her hands out to me. I saw yellow and blue jackets. Patrollers.

I let Jamie grab my hand. I focused on the feel of her hands around my one free one. Then people were all around me. Someone got a rope around my chest, somehow. "Watch out, it's a tree well," I said. I sounded drunk, like my tongue was too thick for my mouth. That made me laugh too.

Things were a bit blurry after that. I remember the toboggan ride. I remember thinking how scared Katy had been. It wasn't so bad. I was only cold though; I hadn't broken anything. Maybe it was different with a broken leg. My brain wasn't working right, but the rest of me seemed okay.

By the time Allison and the other patrollers got me down to the patrol hut, I felt better. Allison insisted on filling in the paperwork for a proper report, which I thought was stupid. While she did that, Jamie told me what had happened. She had been doing a practice run of her own when my board flew out of the trees and nearly took her out.

"I chased it," she said. "When it finally stopped, I recognized your board. The bindings were out...and since it was coming from the trees..."

She didn't seem to want to finish. She sat beside me on the large bench we use for patients. I had a wool blanket wrapped around my shoulders. They'd wanted me to get out of my wet clothes, but I had refused. There was no way I was stripping down in front of everyone, so the heat was on high instead. I was grateful. Being rescued had been humiliation enough for one day.

"Thanks," I said.

"Yeah, well. We've got that shoot tomorrow," she said. Her voice was a little shaky. "I wouldn't want you to skip out again."

Allison was watching. "I think we're done," she said. She smiled. "If you'll just sign here, Ryan?"

I did as she asked, then said goodbye to Jamie. She made me promise to call my aunt and uncle for a ride if I couldn't find Kevin. That night, I didn't mind. I was cold and exhausted and ready to go home.

I decided to change into the dry clothes that I keep in my locker. It took a few fumbles before my fingers remembered the combination. I had it written down at home, but I hardly ever used the locker, so the combination wasn't exactly at the front of my mind.

I opened it and reached for my clothes, then stopped. There was a blue gym bag stuffed in the bottom of my locker. I don't own a blue gym bag.

I looked over my shoulder to make sure no one was watching. I was the only one in the room.

I knelt and pulled the zipper, my hands moving slowly. I smelt it before I even had the bag fully open, the too-sweet smell of weed. Just like in the van.

I slammed the door shut before anyone could see that I had a bag full of weed in my locker.

chapter seventeen

It had to be Kevin. No one else knew my combination.

I was going to call the police. No, I wasn't. I might kill Kevin—I was seriously considering it—but I wasn't going to call the police. Not until I'd talked to him, anyhow. He was in way over his head. He had to be. I remembered how scared he'd been the day of the drug bust at the hill.

If I could convince him to turn himself in, it might all go easier for him. Better than waiting to get caught. And I was sure he would get caught.

Besides, what were the chances of the police believing me? It was my locker.

It was my locker.

Was Kevin trying to frame me?

No. He wouldn't. But maybe he'd given out my locker combination. I could see him doing that. He knew I rarely used the locker. It must have seemed like a good hiding place.

One thing I knew. I couldn't leave the stuff there.

I changed quickly, trying to ignore the fact that my spare clothes smelled like dope just from being in the locker. I threw the gym bag over my shoulder. An idea was starting to form in my head.

The blue gym bag didn't look that different from the bags the Ski Patrol kept in the toboggans, holding all the straps and cervical collars and so on. My patrol armband was in my jacket pocket. I wrapped it around the handle of the gym bag. Anyone from the hill who saw me would think I was carrying a first-aid kit.

I checked my watch. There was time for one more run. I was beyond exhausted, but it's amazing how finding a bag full of dope in your locker will get the old adrenaline pumping.

I put my newly dry feet back into my soaking-wet snowboarding boots. Ugh.

Jamie had taken my board and bindings and promised to have it all fixed up for tomorrow. That was probably one of the nicest things anyone had ever done for me. I had been surprised, not only by her offer, but also by the fact that I accepted it. I had expected not to want to let my board out of my sight, but I trusted Jamie.

How could I not? She had saved my life.

I ducked into the patrol hut to grab the key I needed and to borrow a snowboard from the ski swap stockpile...the same one I had used the day my board got stolen. Then I headed up the hill again, gym bag strapped across my shoulders.

I made my way to a rarely used toboggan cache near the top of one of the easier runs on the hill. Just to be on the safe side, I hauled the toboggan all the way out of the cache, then set the bag in the cache. I used the toboggan to push the bag all the way to the back. Now if someone pulled the toboggan out, they wouldn't get a bag full of weed along with it. No one would know the bag was there unless they looked.

It wasn't like I had taken down the whole snowboard-stealing/drug-dealing operation single-handedly, but I still felt pretty good about myself. I had done something they didn't expect. I had something of theirs. It was a small gesture, but at least it was a gesture.

I was taking a stand.

chapter eighteen

I didn't feel so sure of myself when I got back to the parking lot and realized Kevin had left without me again. That must have been the message I got when I was trapped up in the tree well. With all that had happened, I had forgotten to check.

Lovely. While I was a couple of inches of snowfall away from dying, Kevin was making plans to go out drinking with his scumbag friends.

My adrenaline had worn off a good ten minutes ago. My arms and legs felt rubbery. I phoned my aunt to come pick me up at the hill and sat down right there in the parking lot to wait.

She was unusually quiet on the ride home. Finally, about halfway there, she came out with it. "Is everything all right between you and Kevin?"

It was all right there, on the tip of my tongue. I bit it back. "I guess. Why?"

"He hasn't been home for two nights, Ryan. Did you two have a fight?"

That hurt, probably more than she meant it to. I'm sure that she didn't mean to imply that it was my fault Kevin wasn't coming home, but I knew that it was—if he didn't feel like he needed to avoid my questions, he wouldn't need to stay away. And I also knew, given a choice between their nephew and their son, they'd rather have their son. They were great people, my aunt and uncle, but they weren't my parents.

I missed Mom and Dad suddenly and so fiercely that I found myself blinking very hard and very fast.

Things were messed up. I didn't know what to do. My cousin hated me. Someone had tried to...maybe not to kill me, but that was how it might have turned out.

My aunt was looking at me. "Ryan?"

"It's okay," I said. "I'll talk to him."

She sighed. "It was so much simpler when you two were little, you know?"

I did.

I had no chance to talk to Kevin that evening. He wasn't home by the time I crawled into bed. I left the lamp on, planning to stay alert in case he came home, but honestly, I don't think I lasted two minutes.

I woke up when Kevin shook my shoulder.

"Mmrrrmph?" I said. Or something like that.

"Ryan. Wake up." His breath smelled bad. Beer and garlic.

"All right, all right, I'm awake." I sat up and rubbed my face, trying to get the cobwebby feeling out of my eyes. "What time is it?"

"Dunno. Maybe two." His voice sounded thick, like mine had when the patrollers pulled me out of the tree well. Only I was willing to bet Kevin didn't have hypothermia. "I heard what happened," he said. "Thank god you're okay."

Personally I thought Jamie had more to do with it, but that wasn't a conversation I felt like having. Kevin was looking at me and blinking like he wanted to cry. "Are you drunk?" I asked. Not that I minded, or that it would be the first time, but I wanted to know which Kevin I was dealing with. There seemed to be a lot of different Kevins lately.

He shrugged. "Maybe a little. Listen. I have to talk to you."

"No kidding," I said. "You think? What the hell are you mixed up in, anyhow? Drugs, stealing...I mean, why both? It's like an all-you-can-eat crime buffet. It doesn't even make sense."

He shrugged again. The next time he did that, I was going to deck him, I swear. "Things started small, and then they escalated. I dunno. I'm not the one in charge." He hesitated. "Someone told me you broke into the van. Bad move, cuz."

"Yeah, I figured that out," I said. "Kevin, you've got to go to the police. We can go together. I've got pictures on my phone. These guys are dangerous."

He nodded. "Yeah. They are. And that's why you've got to give it back," he said.

"Give what back?"

"The bag that was in your locker. I know you found it. It had to be you." He had to look at me like I had done something wrong.

"You put that there? Damn it, Kevin!" I smacked the mattress.

"I just needed somewhere safe. They arrested Archie, and I was scared. I was stuck with this bag full of weed—I needed to get rid of it. I panicked and called you, and it was awesome. Just talking to you made me feel better. And then I remembered about your locker...you don't mind, do you?"

I did, obviously, but he'd been drinking. It was better if I let him think we were all chummy for now. We could deal with the hard stuff in the morning. "Yeah, great. Glad I could help." I shook my head. "How'd you get mixed up in this, anyhow?" But I knew the answer. Greed. His new truck, the fact that he always seemed to have money.

"Look, I gotta go," Kevin said. "Just tell me where you hid the bag, okay? There's this guy, he needs it back, or I have to give him the money. I don't have the money." He wasn't looking at me now.

Go? Where was he planning to go at two in the morning? "Yeah, well, that's too bad. Because I'm not telling you."

"C'mon. Just out with it and you can go back to sleep."

"Piss off. I'll tell you where that bag is when we're in front of a police officer and you've got a lawyer to look after you. Oh yeah, and it should be daytime." So much for my plan of letting him think everything was fine.

He grabbed me by the shoulders and shook me. "A lawyer's not gonna help," he said. "Don't be stupid."

I shoved him away. He must have been more than a little drunk, because he crashed down way too easily. I scrambled out of bed and watched while he got to his feet. He stared at me for a few seconds before he lunged. The tackle caught me off guard. We slammed into the closet door together, his shoulder in my gut. A picture fell off the wall and landed facedown. It sounded like the glass shattered.

It hurt to breathe. Kevin had knocked the wind out of me. Not much of a fight, really. I was lying there, curled up and pathetic, trying to get my lungs to work, when my aunt and uncle barged in. "Say anything, and I'll tell them it's you,"

Kevin whispered. "How long do you think they'll let you stay then?"

"What in the blue blazes is going on here?" my uncle yelled.

My aunt swept past him. "Are you all right? Boys? Kevin?"

He stood up, swaying a little. "I was just leaving." He brushed past his mom on the way out.

His dad followed. I heard them shouting in the living room.

My aunt helped me sit up, but she kept looking over her shoulder, at the door.

Kevin's words still rang in my ears. I couldn't believe he would say that to me. But he had a point. If it came down to it, it was his word against mine. I couldn't prove much. The drugs came from my locker. I was the one who knew where they were. And if I was so suspicious, why hadn't I gone to the police earlier? "Worried for my cousin" only counted for so much. Particularly when that cousin had just bodychecked me into the closet. Who would believe me?

My uncle came back in, shaking his head. "He left," he said. "Got past me."

I wanted to tell him not to feel bad. Kevin was getting past a lot of people these days. I hadn't found my voice yet. When I did, it was just a croak. "I don't think I should live here anymore," I said.

chapter nineteen

They made me stay. Even when I wouldn't tell them what was wrong with Kevin, they made me stay. "It's the middle of the night," my aunt had said. "Try to sleep. We'll talk in the morning."

In the morning, I was up and out the door before they woke up. One of the more useful tricks I picked up from Kevin.

It was a long walk to the hill. That was all right. I had time to kill.

It was Saturday. The hill would open at nine. Sweep started at eight, so I waited outside the patrol hut for someone to let me in. Surprise, surprise, it was Allison. Poor Allison. I wondered if she spent all her time patrolling because she had no life, or if she had no life because she spent all her time patrolling.

Like I was one to talk.

I helped them with opening sweep and then grabbed some breakfast from the cafeteria.

Jamie and I were due to meet in the main chalet at 11:00 AM. I waited until five minutes to. I didn't want to spend any more time in there than I had to, in case I ran into Kevin or one of his druggie friends. Today was important. I wasn't going to let anyone ruin it for me.

She was there already, waiting for me. Her board and my board were both leaning against a table. "I didn't want to let them out of my sight," she said. "How do you feel?"

Nervous. Stressed. Alone. But she was only talking about the accident. She didn't know about Kevin or my plans to move out. "Fine," I said. "Thanks for fixing my board."

She studied me—a close-up and serious look that made me feel self-conscious. "I'm just glad you're okay," she said.

"I wouldn't have been," I said. "You—"

She shrugged, but she was smiling. "It's okay. You'd have done the same. Let's go warm up."

We did a few practice runs before meeting Ted. All the way up the lift, he talked to us, telling us what he wanted. "Just have fun. Do what you like to do. Push it a little. I want to see risks, but I want you relaxed. You'll only look relaxed if you're having fun."

To me, it sounded like he wanted a bunch of things that didn't go together. My throat felt dry. I swallowed.

At the top, he pinned little clip-on video recorders on our jackets. "Great angles with these," he said. The idea was that the clip-ons would film the rider's point of view, while his camera guys captured the moves.

"We'll start slow," he said. "Take a couple runs at it. We don't even need to start filming right away."

But he had already done something that made the little green light appear on the my clip-on camera, so I figured if he told us he wasn't filming, it was just to get us to relax.

I was glad that at least we weren't riding near the trees where I had gotten stuck in the well. I never wanted to see that place again. I sure didn't want to be thinking about it now, when I needed to concentrate on my riding. Instead, I looked at the hill Ted had chosen.

The hill here made a bit of a slope. I knew that the mound on the right was a rock, covered in snow, but it made a great natural jump. There was a fallen log on the left just shy of the tree line. It had the barest coating of ice on it. I wondered if that was enough to protect my board if I used it like a rail.

I didn't hit it my first time down. I went for the rock instead and made a pretty decent jump. Just a grab, nothing fancy. I was getting a feel for the distance.

The trouble with back-forty riding is the hike back up the hill after each ride. It wasn't so bad here. We weren't covering that much distance. It was no worse than hanging out on the half-pipe for a few hours, riding down and walking up again and again. I figured there would be longer runs later on. Those might get tougher.

My second time down, I hit the rock again. This time, I went into a twist. I landed switch, rode away clean and turned back to watch Jamie. The second she launched herself off the rock, I knew what she was trying. She started the rotation, but she was slow moving into the flip. Her backside rodeo landed her on her back. She laughed it off and got up again. I was pretty sure Ted liked it. Spills make good footage.

I tried the log rail after that and got in a couple of good slides before my phone rang. I answered it without thinking.

"Ryan?" It was Kevin's voice.

I pulled the phone away from my ear and stared at it. All I had to do was fold it shut. Hang up on him. Let the stupid, selfish bastard see how he liked that.

"Don't hang up!" His voice came out loud and desperate, like he knew what I was about to do. I moved the phone back to my ear.

"Talk," I said.

"I'm in trouble, cuz. This time, I really am. I need you."

Was that a sob? I moved the phone away again to stare at it, but I still heard him say, "Ryan? I think they're going to kill me."

chapter twenty

"That's enough." Another voice came on the line. "Is this Kevin's cousin?"

"Who wants to know?" I said.

"Smart mouth. It'll get you into trouble. Do you watch movies, Kevin's cousin?"

"Are you asking me out?"

"Shut the frig up," he said. Or something like that.

I waited.

"If you watch movies, you know how this goes. You have something I want.

I have something you want. Very basic. You bring my bag, with the weed, to Bridge Run. Leave it there, under the bridge. Ride down to the bottom of the hill and wait for your idiot cousin. I see police or anybody else, you get to spend the rest of your life thinking about how you screwed up. Got it?"

I swallowed. "Bridge Run. Weed for idiot cousin," I said, trying to sound braver than I felt. My hand shook, but he couldn't hear that. "Seems pretty straightforward."

He hung up.

I had lied. It didn't seem straight-forward at all.

I should go to the police. But my dad had done that, and it hadn't exactly helped anything, had it? No. It might not be "doing the right thing," but I was going to get Kevin back, hopefully uninjured. Then I could have the pleasure of beating the crap out of the idiot myself.

Or at least that's what I'd tell him, if he asked. If we came out of this okay. My palms were sweaty. It was hard to concentrate.

Bridge Run was a bad place for snow-boarders. That had to be why Jaws, or whoever it was, had picked it. That long, flat trail...I was going to be seriously slow. The run was isolated too.

I didn't have much choice though. Not that I could see.

I walked the rest of the way up to where Ted and the guys with the cameras were.

Ted looked at me, unimpressed. He already knew something was wrong. "Everything okay?" he asked.

"Not really," I said. "I have to go."

He nodded. "I was hoping this would work out." His tone told me I shouldn't expect any more chances.

I unclipped the camera from my coat and handed it to him. "Me too."

That was when Jamie got there. "What the hell are you doing?"

"Something's come up," I said. It was too much to hope for that she would give up and leave it at that.

"No. Whatever it is can wait for another couple of hours while we finish up here."

Ted just watched, arms crossed.

"It can't wait," I said. "I'm sorry." I left.

I had kept the key to the toboggan cache with me. At least I didn't need to go back to the patrol hut. It was going to take me long enough just to fetch the bag and make it all the way over to Bridge Run.

I picked the most direct route I could to the cache. Luckily, there didn't seem to be any patrollers around when I got there. No one to ask why I was hauling out the toboggan.

Getting the bag out was harder. I had to worm all the way into the cache on my elbows. It was a tight fit. Smelled musty in there too, like the wood had gotten damp and rotted. When I finally got far enough into the cache that I could reach the bag, only my feet hung out the end. I looped the bag's strap around my right forearm.

Then I backed up, one inch at a time, pulling it after me.

It wasn't until I had started sliding the toboggan back into the cache that I came up with anything even resembling a plan. If I did exactly what Jaws wanted, there was no guarantee that he wouldn't hurt Kevin. I needed to have control of something.

I glanced over my shoulder to make sure no one was close enough to see what I was doing. I unzipped the spinal injury pack and the gym bag from the van, and switched some of its contents with the weed. Not all, just some. Then I repacked the toboggan and slid it back into place.

Time to go get Kevin. But first, I wanted to talk to someone I could trust. I wanted to talk to Jamie.

chapter twenty-one

I didn't head straight to Bridge Run after all. I hoped I wasn't being followed. I wanted someone to know where I was, in case things went wrong. Right now, Jamie was the only person on the ski hill that I really trusted.

As it turned out, I didn't have to go all the way to the cliff. Ted and Jamie and the two camera guys were on their way up to the top of the hill.

I ran to them. "This is going to sound crazy—"

Ted interrupted me. "That was some phone call you got, kid." He held up the mini-camera. Of course. It would have been recording the whole time, even while I took the call from Kevin. It had a mike on it; not much of one, but enough. Ted had warned us not to say anything too loud if we could help it. The white noise, like wind and breathing, was easier to edit out if there was no talking.

Jamie looked sheepish. "We couldn't hear the whole thing, only your part. But when you held the phone out and looked at it, I saw that it was Kevin calling. And with what you told me before..."

"You in some kind of trouble?" Ted asked.

We made our plan together. It wasn't that different from what I had already come up with. Ted insisted on calling the police. I didn't want him to, but he and Jamie didn't give me a choice. It wasn't like they needed my permission to make the call. They already had all the information they needed. At least Ted wasn't going to make me wait for the police to get to the hill. He understood that I needed to do this now.

He let me wear the clip-on camera again and helped me hide it in my jacket. That part was my idea. If anything happened to Kevin or me, at least there would be some evidence.

I took a deep breath and headed down to Bridge Run.

The gym bag was heavy across my back. I wasn't used to boarding with something so bulky and heavy. It threw off my balance. When I finally got to the top of Bridge Run, the trail was closed off with orange snow fencing.

I hesitated. Bridge Run doesn't get a lot of traffic at the best of times, but it was still unnerving to slip past that fence, knowing that I wasn't going to encounter anyone else on the trail.

I started down the hill, making the first turn awkwardly because of the bag across my back. The flat part, the bridge, came up fast. Too fast. I stopped just before the bridge. There was a cold, scared feeling deep in my stomach.

This was where I was supposed to leave the drugs. This was where things were going to go right or go wrong.

I dropped the bag. Then I sat down and unstrapped my snowboard. The bag had to go under the bridge. That seemed over-complicated to me, but I guess they didn't want anyone coming across it by accident... although I thought the run being blocked off was probably insurance enough.

I carried the bag off the trail and made my way under the bridge, gripping the metal railings. The drop-off wasn't steep right here, and there was room under the bridge to stash the bag, but the ground dropped away pretty fast after that.

I had to climb on all fours to get up on the trail again. I strapped my board back on, but only one foot, so I could skate. I went halfway across the bridge and waited. This was where my plan veered off from my instructions.

It was only a moment before my cell phone rang. I didn't bother to say hello. "I'm not leaving until I see Kevin," I said.

chapter twenty two

"You'll see Kevin when I get my stuff back," the voice said. "Now get off the trail."

I took another deep breath to steady myself. "I'll move away," I said, "but I'm not leaving without my cousin." I hung up.

I skated over to where the flat part of the trail ended, and then I waited again. I heard his skis scraping across the snow before I saw him.

He saw me, I was sure, but he didn't acknowledge me. He stopped close to where I had been and stepped out of his skis. It had been hard enough monkeying around the bridge with snowboard boots on. Ski boots are harder and more slippery. Truthfully, part of me hoped he would fall. He didn't though. He used his poles to get back up on the trail with the bag. Poles. The one great advantage that skiers have.

He knelt down, right there on the trail, and unzipped the bag. The shiver that ran down my spine had nothing to do with the cold. This was the part where they were going to get angry. I needed to stay calm. If I stayed calm, I just might pull this off.

The man spoke into a radio. Sound travels in winter. I heard him perfectly. "Half the bag is stuffed with bandages," he said.

Whoever was on the other end of the radio swore into the receiver. My cell phone rang a microsecond later.

"You must not care about your cousin very much," a man said when I answered. I was sure the voice belonged to Jaws.

"I do," I said. "That's why I kept half of your stuff back. Now let me see Kevin—unhurt—and I'll tell you where to find it."

There was silence on the other end of the phone. I swallowed. And then I heard Kevin's voice, high and scared. "Cuz, what are you playing at?"

"Trust me," I said. "You'll be fine."

The way I saw it, the sort of criminals who stole boards and sold dope at a ski resort weren't the sort of people who went in for kidnapping and murder. It was too big a leap.

I hoped.

"Just do what they want," Kevin said. "Damn it, why do you have to make everything so complicated?"

It seemed like a weird question coming from someone who was supposedly afraid for his life. "Why do I—? What are you even talking about?"

"You—," Kevin started, but then he was cut off.

"I'm sending him down," Jaws said. "No more tricks."

He didn't want Kevin talking to me. My brain started filling in the blanks. I wasn't sure I liked the picture it made.

Whoever I was dealing with knew that my cousin and I were close. They couldn't know that just from watching. Not lately, anyhow. Lately, we'd been acting like two people who didn't give a crap about each other. They also knew that I wasn't likely to go running to the police. Someone would have to know my family history, and how I felt about what happened to my dad, to make that kind of call about me.

Kevin was in on it. Or at least, he thought he was.

I didn't know whether to be angry or to feel sorry for the idiot.

I waited. It had seemed like it took only seconds for me to board down to where the bridge started. Now, waiting for Kevin, it felt like hours.

When I finally heard them approaching, the sound was wrong. There was the scraping sound of someone snowplowing down the hill, but there were footsteps too. It was another minute or so before I saw them. Kevin was walking in front, his hands tied behind his back. Behind him, on skis, was Jaws, pointing a gun at Kevin.

chapter twenty-three

A gun? My hands got really cold all of a sudden. Stealing, drugs, now a gun. Talk about escalating.

Kevin reached the level part of the hill. Jaws shoved him from behind, and he stumbled. Kevin looked at me but said nothing. His mouth made a tight line across his face.

The whole length of the bridge was between me and them. I could probably make it down the hill before they caught me.

The hill dropped off pretty steeply just a step back from where I was.

I hated that running away had even crossed my mind.

"It's in a patrol bag inside a toboggan cache," I said. "Above the rookie run. I have the key." I held out my hand, key shining against my bare palm. They were going to have to come close to get it.

It wasn't Jaws who moved, though. It was the first guy, the skier who had checked the bag. He skated across the bridge to me. I held still. He snatched the key out of my hand. "You'd better be telling the truth," he said.

I nodded. I was pretty sure I had his face on camera, now, but somehow that wasn't as comforting as I had thought it might be. Not with that gun pointed at Kevin.

He skated back and started to climb up the hill.

"We'll all just wait here until I hear from my friend," Jaws said.

It was the longest fifteen minutes of my life. Finally, Jaws's radio squawked. "Yeah?" he said.

"The kid wasn't lying," he said. "I got it."

"Good," Jaws said.

This was about as far as my plan went. I had a backup, but it wasn't much of one. "So, can we go now?" I asked.

"Not exactly," Jaws said. He hefted the gun.

"You don't want to do that," I said. "That makes this way more serious than it needs to be."

"I hate to break it to you, but it's already serious," he said. "They arrested Archie."

I tried to stay calm. "So what are you still doing here?" I wanted to make it sound like he had options. It didn't seem to me that he was the sharpest ski on the hill, but he was holding a gun, and that made him dangerous.

"Cleaning up the mess!" he said. I had a feeling that Kevin and I were the mess.

"By shooting us." I shook my head. "You don't have to do that. Just go. We won't say anything."

"I'm not stupid, kid. I'm not going to shoot you if I don't have to. No, my friend here is going to take you off the trail and... well, let's say that you're in for a cold night. By the time they find you, I'll be long gone."

I shivered. The run was closed. Maybe he thought he didn't need to kill us. The cold would do it for him. He'd have been right, if I hadn't told Jamie where I was going.

My brain was still churning, trying to come up with a reply, when everything went wrong. Jaws aimed his gun at me. Kevin shoved him. I heard a loud bang. Something tore into my shoulder, knocking me back. It hurt. I dropped to my knees. When I looked down, there was a hole in my jacket.

I couldn't move fast enough. Jaws turned, pointing the gun at Kevin. Then something flew down the hill and knocked Jaws over.

My vision went weird, like the world was made of rubber, and someone was stretching it. My hands were going numb. I fumbled in my coat pocket and pulled out the black plastic garbage bag I had stashed there. My backup plan. Garbage bag equals high-speed sled.

Kevin was running toward me, over the bridge. "Did he get you? Ryan!"

I threw the bag at him. "Go!" I yelled. I felt like I was going to faint, or throw up from the pain. Everything seemed to slow down—my body didn't want to respond, and the garbage bag seemed to take forever to leave my hand and float through the air. Kevin moved just as slowly, throwing himself through the air to catch the garbage bag.

"Come on!" he shouted. He grabbed for me, but I was already falling. He missed. He landed on the makeshift sled and was gone.

"Flying carpet," I said, or tried to. Something wet trickled down my arm. I felt dizzy and tired, and my shoulder burned.

Jaws was climbing to his feet, and even confused as I was, I knew that was a bad thing. I needed to follow Kevin. One boot was strapped into my board already. I felt too woozy to stand, but I knelt on my snowboard and pushed forward. I picked up speed going over the drop-off, just as Kevin had. I was out of control, weaving back and forth, but just ahead, Bridge Run fed into a busier trail. There would be people around. Witnesses. All I had to do was hang on.

The sky, oddly, seemed to be growing dark. And shifting.

I teetered on my board. Somehow I was in a wider, whiter space now, with fewer trees. I heard someone yell. Then I caught an edge, or my arm, or something. I bailed, snow scraping my face as I rolled and slid down the hill. Someone crashed into me.

"Yard sale," I mumbled. It was the last thing I said for a while.

chapter twenty-four

Things got hazy after that. I think I woke up when I was being lifted out of the toboggan and into the patrol hut. I'm pretty sure I heard Allison. "Ryan, can you hear me? Ryan?"

The next thing I remember is being in the hospital. Even before I opened my eyes, there was that bleached-cotton, disinfectant smell, so I knew where I was. My right leg felt heavy and too hot. My shoulder still hurt.

The first person I saw was Jamie. I tried to sit up, but it didn't work out too well. "What's going on?" I asked.

She laughed, but her face was red, like she'd been crying. I tried not to feel smug about that, but I liked that she had been worried about me. "Not much," she said. "The police got the bad guys. He...the bullet grazed your shoulder. The doctor said you'll be okay. And you've got a broken leg. Sorry."

That was why my leg felt so hot and heavy. It had a cast on it. I frowned at it.

"I can sign it if you want," she offered.

"How do you feel, sweetheart?" It was my aunt, stepping closer to the bed so I could see her. She must have been in the room the whole time.

"I'm fine," I said. I tried again to sit up. This time, I managed with my aunt's help. "Where's Kevin?"

She looked down and fiddled with my sheets. "The police had a few things to

ask him," she said. "Your uncle is with him."
Her mouth trembled a bit. I got the feeling
there was more to it. She didn't want to
tell me.

"Do you want to go?" I asked. He was
her son. I was just her nephew.

She smiled at me then, but her eyes
were too bright. "Thank you. No. He'll be
fine. He isn't...Your parents are coming,
dear, did I tell you?"

"Mom and Dad? When?" I felt
Christmas-morning eager all of a sudden.

She glanced at a clock on the wall.
"They should have landed by now," she
said. "I can check, if you like." Her eyes
were bright again, and I wondered if
maybe she just wanted a minute alone.
I would. Better than crying in front of
other people.

"Sure," I said, "that would be great."
I grabbed her hand before she left.
"Thanks." I didn't mean just for checking
on the airplane.

She sniffed and smiled before she left.

"She was worried about you," Jamie said softly, after she was gone.

I looked at her. "It looks like you were upset about something too. Mad that I messed up the video shoot?" I grinned to let her know I was joking.

"That's not it, you goof," she said, and I was sure she was going to admit it then. She had been worried. "My board got mangled when I had to throw it at that guy who shot you."

"Your board?"

"I loved that board." She smiled back, and I knew she was kidding, but that wasn't the part that had me sitting up straight in my bed.

"You threw your board? What were you doing there? Why were you that close? He had a gun!"

She stepped back. "You're welcome."

"What if they'd seen you?"

"I made sure they didn't," she said. "Besides, the police were already on their way."

I didn't like that answer. It was one thing for me to get involved in my cousin's mess. It was different for Jamie.

"I'm sorry about your board," I said finally. It wasn't what I meant to say, but I wasn't sure I had the words for that, yet.

She shrugged and drew a little closer. "I'll live. You too. That's what matters."

My aunt returned just then. "Ryan? There is a woman here from the newspaper. Are you feeling strong enough to talk to her?"

I glanced at Jamie. She nodded. She'd help me get the story straight. "All right," I said.

I think I learned more from the interview than the reporter did. She already had most of the story. I had slept through it. The police had been waiting by the toboggan cache when Jaws' partner checked for the drugs. They apprehended him based on that. Ted's video camera had caught most of what happened on Bridge Run. He had been thrilled until the police told him he couldn't release the footage.

Jamie and I were being talked about as the "snowboarding heroes." Good publicity, if not entirely accurate. I thought we'd mostly been lucky. Things could have turned out a lot worse.

"How about you?" the reporter asked. "Do you plan to continue snowboarding?"

"Absolutely," I said. "And if Ted Travis wants to try that back-forty video again, I'm there. As soon as my leg heals." I thought Ted would be happy with the plug. Maybe happy enough to forgive me for taking off. It wasn't like I hadn't wanted to be there. It was just...some things were more important.

I looked at the clock and wondered when my parents would arrive.

Jamie caught me looking. "I've never met your parents," she said. "What are they like?"

I smiled. "You'll like my dad. He's—" I thought for a minute, searching for a way to describe him. "He always wants to do the right thing, you know? Even if it's stupid and it costs him."

She looked at me strangely. The corner of her mouth twitched up a little.

"What?"

"Nothing, Ryan." She moved closer and took my hand. It felt good. Really good.

I thought about what I had just said, and suddenly I knew why she was smiling. My dad and I are more alike than I ever thought. And that's not a bad thing at all.

Acknowledgments

First of all, I need to thank Travis Tedford for allowing me to pick his brain about all things snowboarding. The character Ted Travis, although not much like the real Travis, is named in his honor. And, although the patrol and hill depicted in this book are meant to represent neither the Canadian Ski Patrol nor the hill I patrolled for five years, I would never have had the idea for this story without the experience of volunteering with CSPS and working with the wonderful people of Lakeridge patrol. Any similarities in characters or events are accidental, but that was where I first had the idea of setting a novel on a ski hill. I'd also like to thank my agent, Lise Henderson (now retired), for bringing me the opportunity to write for Orca Sports and for taking a chance on a new writer, and my editor, Sarah Harvey, for helping make the story so much better. Nora Rock and Cheryl Rainfield both offered invaluable feedback and encouragement on early drafts—thank you, ladies, you're wonderful! Most of all, thank you to my husband, Aaron, for help and encouragement and a million other things.

A mediocre skier with exceptional first-aid skills, Erin Thomas spent five years as a ski patroller, before giving it up to focus on her writing and primary schoolteaching. Erin lives with her family in Whitby, Ontario.